LESLIE RUTH DAMUDE

Hearts of Wax

Contents

Introduction

Inspired by a True Story
Interwoven with Fiction
Accented with Dramatic License

"Poor lady, she were better love a dream
Disguise, I see thou art a wickedness,
Wherein the pregnant enemy does much.
How easy is it for the proper false
*In women's **waxen hearts** to set their forms!*
Alas, our frailty is the cause, not we,
For such as we are made of, such we be."

Twelfth Night, *by William Shakespeare*

Although slavery had existed in a variety of forms for millennia, in the early 16th century Britain's colonial expansion fueled the British Slave Trade, an extremely cruel and efficient form of enslavement. Over the next 300 years, more than 12.5 million Africans were kidnapped by Britain and other colonial powers, packed tightly in the holds of ships, and transported to the Americas and the Caribbean. There they were sold as slaves in exchange for rum, molasses, cotton, and tobacco, which were exported to Britain and Europe.

During the "Middle Passage" from West Africa to the West Indies, 10 percent of the Africans did not survive the voyage; a similar number died within the first year of slavery.

In 1789 **William Wilberforce**, a young Member of Parliament, gave a powerful four-hour speech which was meticulously researched with the help of a committed group of Abolitionist colleagues. *"When I consider the magnitude of the subject which I am to bring before the House ... it is impossible for me not to feel both terrified and concerned at my own inadequacy to such a task ... the end of which is the total abolition of the Slave Trade ... Never, never will we desist till we extinguish every trace of this bloody traffic, which is a disgrace and dishonour to this country."*

But opposition was fierce. Although some British citizens supported the cause of Abolition, there were thousands of British families whose wealth depended on slavery. And so, Wilberforce and his colleagues were often mocked and insulted, and at times physically threatened. Year after year Wilberforce introduced a bill for Abolition of the Slave Trade in the House of Commons. And year after year it was defeated. Until finally, on February 23, 1807, the Abolition Of The Slave Trade Act passed by a huge margin, to the enormous joy of Wilberforce and his colleagues.

Sadly, Abolition did not improve the lives of those who remained enslaved on plantations in the West Indies. Sugar had become the "white gold" that contributed significantly to Britain's prosperity. But growing sugar cane was very labour-intensive, and maximizing profits required dependence on a false economy based on unpaid labour: slave labour. And so, when the fight for **Abolition** of the Slave Trade finally ended in victory in February 1807, the campaign for the **Emancipation** of those still enslaved in the British West Indies had only begun.

Prologue

Pinney Plantation, Nevis, West Indies, February 23, 1807

Black and white. White and black. The keys always seemed to draw Stuart into a different world as they came alive under his fingers. A world that was not so easily marred by the confusing ambiguity that he sensed beneath the surface. A world in which he felt at home.

At the age of fourteen, Stuart showed a remarkable gift for the piano, and played with a depth of feeling far beyond his age. He often seemed drawn to the minor key – perhaps his unconscious reaction to a way of life that still seemed foreign two years after the tragic death of his parents, which had torn him from the tranquil English village where he had been raised.

"Beautiful, Stuart," encouraged his Aunt Lydia, who was sitting beside him on the piano bench. "You certainly have my sister's gift." She had told him many times how much he resembled his mother, not only due to his unusual amber eyes and blonde hair, but also in his inquisitive mind, and quick wit. Yet although his aunt did her best to make him feel like part of the family, his Uncle Malcolm was cold and distant, and treated him like an outsider.

Stuart was tall for his age and thin – no match in physical prowess for his older cousin Vincent, who found it entertaining to insult and harass him. And so, it was perhaps inevitable that Stuart was learning to fight not with fists, but with words.

Suddenly, the loud howling of a pack of dogs – frenzied and out for blood – shattered the peaceful moment. Stuart pulled his hands from the keys and looked toward the door as a slender middle-aged black woman abruptly entered the room, clearly agitated but too breathless to speak.

"What is it, Bess?" asked Lydia.

After catching her breath, the anguished words tumbled from her mouth. "It's Daniel Miss Lydia. They caught 'im and I'm 'fraid they gonna kill 'im!"

Lydia leapt to her feet, her delicate features contorted in alarm, and went with Bess out the front door of the mansion, followed hesitantly by Stuart.

By the time Lydia, Stuart and Bess had walked down the path to the slave quarters, a crowd had gathered in the packed mud square in the center of the huts. The jeering white faces of the slavedrivers, laughing and relishing the entertainment. Downcast black faces, masking their pain and fear - only there because they were given no choice, because they needed to "learn a lesson." Tense with apprehension, Stuart closed his eyes and tried to picture the piano keys. Black and white. White and black. Tried to hear the melody that he had played so recently. Tried to put some order back into his world.

But then they dragged Daniel into the square and tied him to the post, and Stuart knew that he could not do it. There was no order. The melody was gone, and he could not find it again. And reluctantly he opened his eyes and watched as these cruel men tied the escaped slave to the whipping post – and as the huge muscular arms of the slavedriver began to lash him with the whip.

Daniel's mother Sarah, her weathered face distorted in agony, moaned as she rocked back and forth on her knees at the front of the crowd. Stuart's uncle, Malcolm Bartley, the manager of the plantation, stood impassively behind her, unmoved by the old woman's distress. And then Lydia approached her husband and with a gentle hand on his arm pleaded, "Malcolm, he has been punished enough!"

Malcolm shook his arm free of his wife's hand, and completely ignored her. Turning to the slave drivers he commanded, "Sell him!"

"No Massa," Sarah begged. "Please don't sell 'im. Please Massa ..."

Malcolm did not even look at the grieving mother and turned toward the house.

"You can't do this," Lydia pleaded. "On his last visit John Pinney said he wants the slaves to be treated fairly."

But her husband only stared at her coldly and replied, "A profitable plantation requires compliant slaves. And since Pinney is unlikely to make the sea voyage from England again with his young family, I will continue to act on his behalf as I see fit!"

As Malcolm walked away from Lydia, Stuart's loyalty to his aunt began to waver. For despite his uncle's coldness and cruelty, Stuart knew that he would do almost anything to earn his approval.

Sarah wailed loudly as the slavedrivers dragged Daniel away. Lydia walked over and put her hand gently on her shoulder, trying to convince her to go into her hut. But Sarah's grief was raw and deep and would not be silenced. Concerned for his aunt, Stuart began to walk toward her.

"You're too old for this, Stuart!" sneered his cousin Vincent, who came up behind him and grabbed his arm.

"Vincent, leave him alone!" Lydia implored, but he ignored her.

Picking up a lamp, Vincent pushed his cousin ahead of him, between the slave huts. "Come on Stuart. I'll make a man of you!"

Vincent stopped in front of a hut where Rachel, a beautiful young slave, was preparing food over a fire. There was a visceral expression of fear on her face that made Stuart feel queasy. He wanted to turn around and run, away from the hut, away from his cousin, but Vincent was much stronger, and he knew there was no escape. Vincent leered at Rachel and motioned her into the hut with a nod of his head, then pushed Stuart in after her.

Vincent put the lamp on the floor near a sleeping mat, then forced Rachel onto the mat. Stuart tried to turn away, but Vincent gripped him by the arm and forced him to watch.

When Vincent began what he came for, Stuart's eyes widened briefly in shock, his pupils dilated. And then he squeezed them tightly shut and tried to find his place of refuge. Black and white. White and black. His fingers on the keys. The haunting melody in a minor key, floating out through the open window over the palm trees ... But when the sound of ripping fabric assaulted his ears, he involuntarily opened his eyes and was initiated into a world that both repelled and captivated him. A world in which the black and white certainty that he had sought was shrouded in shades of grey. And although he did not know it then, it was a moment that would change his life forever.

London, England, February 23, 1807

The shadows shifted across the wall – a chaotic duel between light and dark. And when Lizzie squinted her eyes and tilted her head, she could imagine herself in the midst of the battle. "There are still dragons to slay," Father often told her, and she knew he meant more than the fearsome creatures with sharp claws and fiery breath that lurked in her fantasy world.

Her fingers ran over the surface of the brooch that she had pinned to her nightgown. The image of a kneeling slave was a reminder that even at the age of seven, she too had a part to play.

Why are they taking so long? Lizzie wondered, sitting up in bed and swinging her feet to the floor. She walked across to the window and pressed her nose against the frosty glass. Frustrated by the limited view, she undid the latch and pushed the window wide open. Snow was falling gently, softening the dark outline of the Parliament Building that loomed across the deserted square.

"Lizzie! What are you doing?" hissed her older sister Barbara, throwing back her blankets on the other side of the double bed. "It's freezing out there!"

"They should be done by now!"

"Father said the debate could take hours," Barbara reminded her.

The soft thud of bare feet running along the hallway heralded the entrance of their brothers William, age 10, and Robert, who had recently turned 6.

"You're making a lot of noise!" William whispered.

Touching her brooch absent-mindedly, Lizzie replied, "I want to see Father after ..."

"You're not supposed to wear that to bed!" Robert interrupted loudly.

With arms crossed and chin raised, Lizzie replied defiantly, "I am going to wear it till the slaves are all free!"

"Come on," William interrupted, reaching over to close the window. "We can see better from the library."

The children raced noisily down the corridor and banged open the library door.

"Shh!" scolded Barbara. "You'll wake the baby! And Mrs. Knowles!"

For a few moments, voices were muffled to whispers as the four children crowded around the French doors to the balcony.

"Look!" Lizzie exclaimed, pulling open the doors. "I can see them!"

William pushed past her onto the balcony and pointed at the men who were emerging from Parliament. Barbara peered past William's shoulder and began to laugh as she saw them frolicking happily in the snow like schoolboys. "I can see Uncle James. And cousin Henry. It must be good news! They look so happy!"

"And there is Father!" Lizzie smiled, pointing at the familiar figure in the midst of the celebration, his face beaming with joy.

"They won the vote!" Barbara exclaimed, grabbing Lizzie in a big hug. William and Robert clapped each other excitedly on the back. "The Slave Trade is defeated!"

Their elation was interrupted as their plump middle-aged housekeeper entered, carrying their infant brother Samuel. "What is all the commotion?" she frowned. "When Master Wilberforce gets back …"

"Look Mrs. Knowles!" Barbara urged, pointing to the jubilation in the square. "They won the vote! Father's bill passed! The Slave Trade is over!"

Briefly speechless, Mrs. Knowles shook her head in surprise, then joined the children in their revelry. And as the snow continued to fall gently, Lizzie thought happily that the world seemed different somehow – clean and new and full of possibility.

Chapter 1

Wilberforce Estate, Highwood Hill, England, January 5, 1827 – Twenty Years Later

"Do you think you will be warm enough Lizzie? It is such a cold night!"

"I will be fine, Mother," Lizzie replied, barely concealing her irritation, as she wrapped a red woolen scarf around her neck and pulled on matching gloves.

"I hope you will not be too late," her mother fussed.

"I will be with Charlotte and Alison and their husbands. They will bring me home safely."

With relief, Lizzie caught sight of the Talbot's carriage through the parlour window and quickly descended the front steps to join her friends. Charlotte and Alison made room for Lizzie to sit between them. After the required pleasantries with John and Henry, the three friends left them to their dull business discussion and were soon absorbed in a lively conversation of their own.

"I have a feeling about tonight, Lizzie," whispered Charlotte with an elfish grin.

"A feeling?"

With a wink at Alison, Charlotte replied, "It is, after all, Twelfth Night."

Lizzie frowned with mock suspicion. "And?"

"'Tis a night when anything can happen!"

"What did you have in mind?"

"My cousin Hadley will be there!"

"Hadley!" Lizzie wrinkled her nose in disgust. "Don't you dare!"

As Charlotte exchanged a mischievous glance with Alison, Lizzie's stern frown soon dissolved into contagious laughter. John and Henry stared at the three friends quizzically, mystified by their amusement.

* * *

The Fairfax mansion glittered with light, inside and out, and the vibrant colours of high society fashion. Lizzie handed her coat to a footman, then followed Alison and Charlotte up the elegant staircase to a large salon that had been decorated in rich shades of purple, crimson and gold. Before Lizzie could follow her friends to the beautifully appointed refreshment table, she noticed an elderly woman walking toward her. "Miss Wilberforce, it is so good to see you. You know how I admire your father."

Although Lizzie did not relish a long conversation with one of her father's admirers, she smiled at the kind-hearted old woman and replied politely, "Good evening, Lady Cox. I know Father always speaks highly of you."

With a flush of pleasure, Lady Cox replied, "How is your father's health? There have been rumours."

Lizzie hesitated awkwardly, searching for words to convey the courage with which her father faced his physical trials, without revealing too much. "He is always filled with good humour and his usual wit, despite his challenges," she replied as diplomatically as she could.

"And what of his involvement in the Cause …?" Lady Cox began, but her inquiry was interrupted by the arrival of Charlotte.

"Good evening, Lady Cox," she smiled. "I hope you don't mind if I borrow Lizzie. There is someone who is anxious to meet her."

"Just in time," Lizzie giggled. As her friend led her across the room, Lizzie recognized several men who observed her coldly. She knew they were not admirers of her father, and still resented the personal financial losses that

2

had resulted from the defeat of the Slave Trade.

"Lizzie, you must meet Mary Ames and Betsey Baillie. They are sisters – both widows, and I think you will find them very agreeable."

Lizzie liked both women, who were a few years older than her, and discovered that they had many interests in common. They lived in Bath and were enthusiastic about a school for poor children that they supported there. Lizzie shared the experience of her godmother, Hannah More, who was involved with a similar venture. But then she noticed an awkward young man heading toward them. Hadley! Charlotte had been serious, despite the disaster of their last encounter! With a hurried farewell to her new friends, and a promise to meet soon for tea, Lizzie turned abruptly and headed toward the sound of lively music that drifted from a smaller room at the far side of the salon.

The atmosphere was jovial, with guests crowded around the piano to sing along with the music. Lizzie observed with amusement that several young women hovered near the pianist, a tall, handsome man with blonde hair and riveting amber eyes, and seemed to be vying flirtatiously for his attention.

"You play so beautifully, Stuart," fawned a raven-haired debutante, placing a delicate hand on his shoulder. "Where did you learn to play like that on your tropical island?"

"*Tu joues avec une telle passion!*" intruded a vivacious coquette, leaning close enough that the rich indigo of her embroidered bodice would accentuate her obvious assets. "*As-tu d'autres passions?*" The alluring intimacy of her fluent French left no doubt about her meaning. When the young woman whispered in his ear, Lizzie looked away, unsettled by the sensual smile that flitted across his face.

And then for a moment she exchanged a glance with a man who was standing behind Stuart. A young man with wavy auburn hair and dark blue eyes, who did not seem amused when Stuart quipped, "Charles, do you think I should accept her kind offer?"

"You must be exhausted after your arduous voyage," Charles countered. "And barely recovered from the fever ..."

"I appreciate your concern," Stuart interrupted, "but I feel much better with such stimulating company! It was good of you to invite me to meet your friends."

"I would gladly nurse you back to health, Stuart," teased a petite redhead with sparkling green eyes.

Lizzie noticed that Charles seemed uncomfortable with the exchange. Then, with a slight shrug of his shoulders, he turned around and made his way through the crowded room toward the door.

"Lizzie! How wonderful to see you!" The condescending voice of Agatha Bexhall pulled Lizzie's attention away from the group around the piano.

"Good evening, Agatha. Congratulations on your engagement."

"Yes, Father is very pleased about the match," she preened. "Very advantageous."

Lizzie braced for what she knew was coming and was not surprised when Agatha arched her perfect eyebrows and added in a patronizing tone, "Roderick has a cousin. It would be my pleasure to introduce you."

"Do not go to any trouble on my account," Lizzie replied, barely containing her anger.

With a knowing smile, Agatha's eyes swept over Lizzie's simple dress and commented, "Such a becoming dress. I wore one like it last season to Frances Buckingham's garden party." Her gaze then fixed on the brooch which Lizzie had pinned to the bodice of her dress. "But of course, Lizzie, you are so loyal to your father's Cause. What is it they call it? Emancipation? Quite in his shadow. What young man could compete with that!"

Lizzie was briefly speechless, but before she could reply Agatha waved dismissively and headed toward an ostentatiously dressed woman more worthy of her time.

The entrance of their hostess, Margaret Fairfax, commanded the attention of all the guests. "The performers are approaching," she announced. "Dress warmly everyone, and let the festivities begin!"

* * *

Bundled in their warmest clothes, Lizzie linked arms with Alison and

Charlotte and descended the steps of the mansion to the snowy square below. There was a carnival atmosphere as the party guests joined local villagers who had come to see the traditional Twelfth Night play.

"Look, they're coming! The Mummers!" a young boy pointed excitedly, as the troupe of traveling actors approached. Overcome with laughter, Lizzie and her friends jumped back when the Broomer swept the audience aside with his broom.

"He's here, George of Cappadocia," Charlotte giggled, as a gaudily dressed knight entered jauntily on a hobby horse, flourishing a wooden sword.

On the other side of the lively crowd, Lizzie noticed the young man, Charles, and could not keep herself from staring. But when for a moment their eyes met, she blushed and quickly looked away. As the battle between St. George and the Turkish Knight reached its climax, Lizzie was caught up with the cheers and laughter of the audience. And when the crowd began to disperse, she found herself in the centre of a group of villagers that was walking away from the Fairfax mansion. She turned around and noticed that Alison and Charlotte were walking with other guests back to warm themselves with enticing refreshments and refined conversations. Lizzie considered joining them but realized that she felt more comfortable with these poor peasants in their ragged clothes than with the vanity and pretension of high society. And so, she continued to walk with them, enjoying the high spirits of the children and the cheerful musical accompaniment of a lively fiddler and an old man playing an accordion.

Several children linked hands and began to dance, and a cheerful red-cheeked girl pulled Lizzie into the circle. "Hold on tight, Miss, and don't let go!" Round and round, faster and faster they danced, until Lizzie was out of breath with laughter when the song ended.

A gangly lad in shabby clothes bowed gravely to Lizzie and held out his hand. "Would you dance with me Miss?" She accepted with a gracious smile and followed his clumsy attempts to lead her in a unfamiliar folk dance. Then, from out of the shadows, a dark figure appeared and tapped on the shoulder of Lizzie's partner to cut in on the dance. When Lizzie recognized Charles' enigmatic smile, her feet seemed frozen in place – but the children tried to cajole her into accepting his offer.

"Go ahead Miss!" called a gap-toothed boy in the crowd. "He won't bite!"

"He's a handsome one, Miss! And so polite!"

With a cheeky grin her recent partner added, "And I'll be here to keep an eye on 'im Miss!"

Mortified at being the centre of so much attention, Lizzie was tempted to turn around and run back to the Fairfax's home. But the amused expression on Charles' face held a challenge that she could not resist. And so, she accepted his hand, and allowed him to lead her in a fast-paced reel – as the exuberant onlookers clapped and called out encouragement and advice.

When the song ended, Lizzie smiled awkwardly at her partner, and waved cheerfully at the villagers. But before she could take her leave, several children began to rush past her in a chain, and she was pulled along behind them. In an instant that changed everything, Charles grabbed her hand and followed the laughing column of urchins out onto the snowy field. When a snowball hit Lizzie on the back, a young boy with a lopsided grin laughed at her cheerfully. Without hesitation, Lizzie pelted him back, her arm strong and her aim true.

Within moments there were snowballs flying in all directions, as children and adults joined the rollicking battle. Lizzie noticed with an odd twinge of pleasure that Charles was in the thick of the game, obviously enjoying himself. When he lobbed a snowball at her, she hurled a volley back at him, with the majority easily hitting their mark. With an impish grin, Charles aimed back at her with impressive force and accuracy.

When several children began to make snow angels, Lizzie glanced at Charles laughing at their antics – his expression open and free for the first time since Lizzie had met him. But when their eyes met, she became self-conscious under his penetrating gaze, and looked up at the twinkling stars scattered across the ebony canvas of the night sky.

"The magic of Twelfth Night," she whispered.

"Manners and introductions forgotten," Charles smiled.

With mock formality, Lizzie curtsied and replied, "Elizabeth. My friends call me Lizzie."

"No last name?"

"It is a night for mystery," she laughed.

"My name is Charles," he responded, with a polite bow. Then, with a charming smile, he took Lizzie's gloved hand in his and kissed it. She could feel the blood rush to her cheeks as he held her gaze with an intensity that took her breath away. And although she knew that the magic would soon fade, she wished that she could hold onto this moment forever.

* * *

"A snowball fight?" scolded Charlotte, as they waited in the carriage for the men to join them. "What were you thinking?"

"I have four brothers," Lizzie shrugged.

"But you do not even know his last name!"

"It only seemed fair. I did not offer mine."

"But why Lizzie?" Alison asked gently.

"You know what always happens. As soon as they hear the name Wilberforce."

"But what will your parents say?" Alison persisted.

"They will say nothing at all," Lizzie replied, barely above a whisper, "because I will never see Charles again."

"Never?"

"I left my stories of handsome princes and magic spells in the nursery long ago."

Chapter 2

Bristol, England - Two Weeks Later

"We're going to be late," Charles fumed, as the clock that towered above the square struck one. "Stuart knows how important this meeting is!"

"There he is," replied his associate, Gerald, as Stuart's tall, elegant figure appeared around the corner.

"I was sorely tempted to send my regrets," Stuart quipped, with no apology for his tardiness. "The odds on King-Maker are 30 to 1!"

Charles did not take the bait and hailed the next carriage that passed by. "We must make a stop on the way," he informed them, as they clattered over the cobblestones.

"Where?" asked Gerald in surprise.

"A charity event for a cause that I support. My sisters are visiting from Bath for a few days to help out and I have invited some influential friends."

"Of course," Stuart goaded. "With your political ambitions you must take advantage of every opportunity!"

"The National School Committee does very important work!" Charles retorted. "Without it many poor children in England would have no education at all!"

"Please forgive my ignorance," Stuart implored in a contrite tone that did not quite ring true.

Charles stared back at him uneasily, wondering what darker passions lurked beneath his flippant veneer.

* * *

The books were obviously cast-offs, with yellowed pages and tattered covers. Lizzie wrinkled her nose as she blew the dust off a basketful of volumes that had probably sat in a neglected attic for years. "Some of these would be best used as fuel for the fire!" she frowned, wiping her soiled hands on her apron.

Alison was flipping through the pages of a children's picture book. "Maggie would like this one," she responded, as she tucked the book into the pocket of her apron and put a coin into the cash box.

"Well, if you are going to buy one before the patrons arrive, then so will I," Lizzie smiled, picking up a book that had already been stacked for sale, and dropping in a coin.

"Twelfth Night?" Alison inquired.

Lizzie shrugged casually, then gestured toward Betsey Baillie and Mary Aimes, the widowed sisters that she had first encountered at the Fairfax gala. She had met them for tea since then and they had invited her and Alison to join them as volunteers for a charity that their brother supported. Since Alison had a cousin who lived in Bristol, she and Lizzie had arranged to stay with her. Observing that Betsey and Mary had already finished setting up tables with baked goods and hand-crafted items Lizzie urged, "We had better finish with this book table before everyone arrives."

"Lizzie, I will finish up here. You need to find a mirror to make yourself presentable," Alison chided, as she handed her a clean handkerchief. "You have dust on your face and your apron."

There was a small looking glass in the cloakroom, and Lizzie quickly wiped her face and removed the apron. As she straightened her plain light green dress, her fingers brushed against her brooch. The brooch she always wore – would always wear – until …

"Hurry Lizzie!" Alison urged, interrupting her thoughts. "They need us to serve punch at the refreshment table." Teasing one another good-naturedly, the two friends linked arms, and took their place just in time to serve the first customer.

* * *

When they entered the parish hall, Charles was pleased to see that many wealthy and fashionable patrons had responded to his invitation. Stuart and Gerald were quickly surrounded by a lively group of attractive young ladies. Although Charles would have preferred to join them, he felt it was important to mingle with the guests and to encourage their generosity. Conversations inevitably revolved around business, and he became trapped in a tedious debate between a portly old man who was an influential merchant and a balding young banker known for his extreme opinions. When his sister Mary waved to him, Charles tactfully took his leave and joined her.

"Charles, come and have some punch," Mary urged, "and I will introduce you to Miss Wilberforce. Betsey and I so enjoy her company."

As he followed his sister to the refreshment table, Charles was startled when he noticed a young woman who was serving punch. His breath caught when he recognized her. The woman he had met at the Twelfth Night gala. That brief but memorable encounter.

"Lizzie, this is my brother Charles Pinney," Mary smiled. "Charles lives here in Bristol, but often visits Betsey and me in Bath. Charles, this is our good friend Elizabeth Wilberforce."

As Lizzie looked up at him her cheeks flushed with a rosy glow. And then, with graceful formality, she responded, "It is good finally to meet you Mr. Pinney. Your sisters have told me so much about you. And of your commitment to this worthy cause."

"It is an unexpected pleasure to make your acquaintance, Miss Wilberforce," Charles replied tentatively.

Mary watched the exchange with an enigmatic smile, then offered helpfully, "Lizzie, it is my turn to take over from you so that you can also enjoy some refreshment." And without waiting for a reply Mary guided Lizzie from behind the table toward Charles.

He led her to a less crowded spot then turned to her with a smile. "The mystery has been solved."

"Mystery?"

"The identity of the Lady of Twelfth Night!"

Lizzie looked down awkwardly and began to finger a brooch which Charles noticed for the first time. He had seen similar jewelry before. A Wedgwood medallion of a kneeling slave, worn by abolitionists. And then, in a voice so faint that it was barely audible, she whispered, "Elizabeth Wilberforce - a name that is too big for me."

Charles stared at Lizzie, sensing her ambivalence, then replied with a comical bow, "'Tis an honour to meet you, Miss Wilberforce." And impulsively, with a warmth that broke through his usual reserve he declared, "You have often filled my thoughts since that enchanted evening. And I am determined not to let you vanish so easily again!"

When Lizzie stared up at him in wide-eyed confusion, Charles feared that his impertinence had ended any chance he had of knowing her better. But she did not turn away, and her reply was soft but equally bold. "You have filled my dreams as well."

A look of understanding passed between them. And as he looked into her eyes, he saw something there that caused his pulse to quicken. She blushed under his gaze but did not look away.

* * *

The carriage ride to the West India Association meeting was short but unpleasant.

"She is smitten with you, Charles," Stuart needled.

"Stay out of it!" Charles snapped.

Ignoring him, Stuart continued, "Such perfect irony. The Abolitionist's daughter! You are far more cunning than I realized!"

"Cunning? I did not anticipate ..."

Recognizing the challenge in Stuart's eyes Charles cut short his reply and turned toward the window. But as usual Stuart was not easily distracted.

With a flourish he reached into his pocket, removed a coin, and displayed it on his palm. "I will wager five guineas that you cannot convince Miss Wilberforce that you are an admirer of her father!"

"Don't be a fool!" Charles exploded. "This is not your concern!"

With an insolent smile Stuart replied, "Please excuse my impertinence. I am merely your employee, and I live to serve."

Pulling a file from a leather satchel, Charles tried to settle his mind to prepare for the upcoming meeting. It was important work since Bristol's prosperity depended on defeating the antislavery lobby. But he found it impossible to concentrate as Stuart regaled Gerald with embellished tales of his recent voyage to England. In truth, Charles mused, there was no need for exaggeration. The ship had been buffeted by fierce storms that had delayed arrival in Bristol for almost a month. And when they had finally docked, Stuart was still weak from the effects of a high fever that had confined him to his bunk for over a week. And so, although Stuart was his employee, Charles had invited Stuart to stay with him for a few days so that he could regain his strength. It was not until the Twelfth Night gala that Charles realized that this blurring of the boundary between employer and employee had been a mistake – especially for a man as resistant to authority as Stuart proved to be.

Charles regretted that so much would depend on the testimony of this mercurial man since Charles, like many other merchants who owned plantations, had never visited the West Indies. But there was no denying Stuart's gift for eloquent rhetoric that could grip the attention of even the most uncongenial audiences. And although at times he seemed to take perverse pleasure in shocking his listeners, it was perhaps this very unpredictability that made him most effective.

Although Stuart had moved to his own lodgings, he continued to disrupt the calm orderliness of Charles' life. But Stuart's cousin Vincent Bartley, who had managed Charles' inheritance capably since the death of Malcolm Bartley three years earlier, had written of Stuart's talents, and had personally vouched for his value to the Association. And although Charles would be glad to see Stuart board one of Charles' ships back to Nevis, there was much to do in the next few months, and he would simply have to find a way of accommodating Stuart's foibles.

Chapter 3

Russell Plantation, Nevis, West Indies, January 1827

At the sound of the bell, Tamar set down her hoe and stretched the knotted muscles in her shoulders. She removed her kerchief to wipe the sweat from her face, then tied back her long wavy chestnut-coloured hair. Joining a file of exhausted slaves, she made her way between the rows of sugar cane onto the packed dirt path that led to their quarters.

And there he was, waiting for her as always. Joseph. Tall and strong, and so handsome that even though four years had passed since the preacher said the words over them, her body still tingled at the sight of him.

"What takin' you so long woman?" he teased, lifting her off the ground and swinging her around.

"Now what our friends thinks of you, Joseph?" she bantered, to the amusement of a stooped old woman and her son who were walking nearby. "Not even waitin' till we gets home to get yo' hands on me!"

"They be right 'bought that," he laughed, as he set her down gently. "They sho' be right."

"But right now, she chided playfully, "I be wantin' yo' hands to fetch me some firewood if you be wantin' yo' supper."

"Yes'm," Joseph grinned, turning toward the woodlot. "My hands is all yours."

Tamar's friend, Elsie, caught up with her, and they chatted lightheartedly as they headed toward the ramshackle collection of broken-down huts that they called home. As they passed the lane that led up to the Massa's Big House, Tamar noticed Massa Russell talking with a tall, thin man who was sitting on a horse. When she saw his intense blue eyes staring at her, she looked away, and tried to quicken her pace. But it was too late.

"Who is this mulatto, John? Call her over. I want a closer look."

When the Massa didn't answer right away, Tamar tried to keep walking with her friends. But then he called her, with a voice that sounded sad and almost like he was sorry. "Tamar, could you come over here?"

Elsie looked back with a worried look but had no choice but to leave Tamar behind. And so, quivering inside, with her eyes fixed on the ground, she stood silently before the stranger.

Reaching over, he pulled off her kerchief and tossed it on the ground, so that her hair fell onto her shoulders. Without thinking, Tamar met his gaze, barely able to hide her anger. "Look at her, John! That creamy skin. Those flashing green eyes. She's no field slave!"

"You can imagine, Vincent, that my wife does not want her to work in the house."

The man stared at her with an expression on his face that made her feel sick inside. She had seen other men look at her like that. And then he laughed. Not a happy laugh, but an ugly laugh that filled her with shame. "Sell her to me. I would never waste her tending sugar cane!"

"I have no plans to sell any of my slaves, Vincent. And Tamar has a husband and a child. I never separate families."

When she heard Massa Russell's reply, Tamar breathed a sigh of relief. But then the stranger, Massa Vincent, said something that made Massa Russell frown and look upset. "But you have some debts, don't you John?" And as he turned his horse to ride away, he added, "Don't forget my offer. When you need to sell her, I'll give you a good price!"

And then he was gone, and when Tamar looked at Massa Russell, the look on his face made her very afraid. For a moment, he hesitated, and Tamar thought he might say something. That he would tell her that Massa Vincent

15

was wrong. That there was no need to fear. But then he turned and walked back to the Big House, without saying a word.

It was 3-year-old Micah who pulled her from her anxious thoughts, as he ran toward her, calling "Mama, Mama," and threw himself into her arms. And with his cheerful smile and excited chatter, she pushed her worries aside and let him lead her home.

* * *

When tentative rays of sunlight began to filter through the window of their tiny hut, Tamar glanced toward Micah on his straw mattress in the corner. Still asleep. She was glad that her restless night had not woken him. When she rolled onto her back, Joseph was watching her. He began to run his finger along her cheek, and then her neck. When he kissed her, she responded, but then pulled away and sat up with a smile. She had not told him about what happened and was afraid he would read it in her face, in her touch.

"The bell will ring ..."

But he just smiled back at her and began to kiss her shoulder, where her nightgown had slipped down. Tamar glanced at Micah, who was still sound asleep. And her fears and resistance melted away as she let Joseph pull her back onto the mattress.

Chapter 4

A Rented Town House in Bath, England, April 1827

Lizzie loved her uncle, James Stephen, who was a close friend and colleague of her father. And she had grown up with Tom Macaulay, whose father Zachary Macaulay had also worked with her father for many years. Lizzie always enjoyed Tom's visits and considered him to be one of her most trusted friends. But their arrival just after dinner, instead of the following day as expected, had thrown her plans into disarray. Her mother was already fussing about where to put all the visitors, since her older brother William had arrived earlier in the week with his wife Mary and 6-year-old son, William Junior, for an unplanned visit. The Highwood Hill house that her parents had bought two years previously was much larger, but had required endless repairs, and they had been forced, once again, to find temporary accommodation.

Of course, Lizzie could not leave without greeting Uncle James and Tom, but she was already late. And she wanted to avoid unwelcome questions about her destination. *I hope Alison will wait for me,* she worried, as she covered her stylish satin gown with a velvet cloak. She descended the stairs slowly, as Uncle James' strong Scottish accent, and equally forceful opinions, emerged from the drawing room. "Ach, Tom! That kind of hot-headedness could undo the gains we've made since Abolition!"

Tom's reply, although more tactful, was equally firm. "The slaves are not much closer to freedom than they were twenty years ago!"

Lizzie hesitated at the bottom of the stairs, waiting for a lull in the conversation.

"Your ideas won't mean much, Tom, until you finish your training for the bar, and win a seat in Parliament!" challenged Uncle James.

Lizzie smiled when her father intervened with his usual warmth and humour. "I've had my share of scolding from James over the years, Tom! Always well-deserved I fear!"

"Well deserved indeed," Uncle James replied with mock irritation, which was soon followed by a wave of laughter.

The arrival of Mrs. Knowles with a tray of tea and pastries signaled an appropriate time for Lizzie to enter the room. She greeted the visitors warmly but declined her mother's offer of tea. Her nephew William was playing with toy soldiers on the floor as a small calico kitten tried to knock them over with her paw. With a mischievous wink Lizzie's father broke off a piece of pastry for his grandson, even though the lad's face was already smeared with fruit filling. When her brother William entered the room and scooped his son up onto his shoulders to take him to bed, Lizzie took advantage of their exit to make her own, promising a longer visit the following day.

As she stopped in front of the mirror in the foyer to put final touches to her hair, Tom asked her father, "Do you miss politics?"

His reply was wistful, yet devoid of self-pity. "I would still be in there fighting if it weren't for my health."

"I don't miss it," Uncle James interjected. "Parliamentary debates that tied your conscience in knots, and your gut along with it!"

"But the House had a fascinating cast of characters!" her father responded warmly. "Drama, and comedy, that could rival the best of theatre!"

Lizzie hesitated, affection for her father causing her to question her decision. But pushing aside her misgivings, she opened the door and hurried down the stairs, her mind filled with anticipation.

* * *

She could see the intensity in his eyes and feel it in his touch, her senses aroused by his closeness. His movements were bold yet gentle, and her skin tingled where his hand touched her waist. His laughter and playful banter chased away any twinges of guilt, and she had no choice but to respond.

When she stumbled slightly, Charles held her more firmly, continuing to sweep her around the dance floor as if nothing were amiss. "Just follow my lead," he smiled.

"I never learned to waltz. Mother felt it was too … improper," Lizzie blushed, fumbling for words, "with men and women so … close."

"Then my duty is clear," Charles laughed.

"You'll guide my steps?"

"If you'll let me."

"And if I follow?"

"There are many things I want to teach you," he enticed, as his eyes swept over the shimmering green folds of Lizzie's dress with an expression that took her breath away.

But as they continued to dance, the spell was broken when Lizzie became aware that she was the subject of scrutiny and ridicule, as several of the elegantly dressed guests gossiped about her with no attempt to lower their voices.

"I cannot believe she came here with him!"

"What perfect irony!"

"Do you think her family knows?"

"They will soon!"

"I would love to see the expression on her father's pious face!"

Humiliated, Lizzie pulled away from Charles, wanting to flee from the room. But suddenly, to her relief, Alison was at her elbow, and Lizzie gratefully followed her into a quiet alcove where they could talk.

"They were gossiping," Lizzie blurted, close to tears. "So cruel, and hateful!"

"Yes, I heard," Alison replied quietly. Then, after an awkward silence, she asked, "Do you think it was wise to come here with him? You know how some people love to stir up scandal."

"It is none of their business!"

"That only whets their appetite!"

Lizzie frowned and began to turn away, but Alison put a gentle hand on her arm. "Lizzie, are you sure about this? That he is right for you?"

"How can you ask that?" Lizzie replied defensively.

"I don't want to see you get hurt."

A tender smile softened Lizzie's face. "If only you knew him. There is something about him. A yearning ..."

"But his business ..."

"I have already seen a change in him," Lizzie insisted.

She could read the doubt and concern in her friend's face, and was relieved when Alison linked arms, with a reassuring smile, and accompanied her back into the ballroom. Together, they walked with heads high past the tattlers, to join Charles, who had been cornered by a jovial old man who was laughing with great hilarity at his own feeble attempts at humour.

At a break in the conversation, Charles excused himself and whispered, "I think we both need some fresh air." As he led her toward the garden, several guests smiled and nodded, but Lizzie wondered anxiously what they would say behind her back.

The garden was a magical place, with candles and exotic Chinese lanterns casting vivid splashes of colour over cobblestone paths and terraced flowerbeds. The scent of lilacs perfumed the air and music from the ballroom drifted through the open French doors.

Lizzie noticed several couples strolling nearby and did not hesitate when Charles took her hand and led her, with an air of mystery, to a more secluded part of the garden, where an ornate wrought-iron lantern illuminated the orange flashes of goldfish in a decorative pond.

"I have something for you," he smiled, holding out a small box and placing it on her palm. When she lifted the lid, light reflected in rich hues of violet-blue from a lovely sapphire, set in a delicate gold filigree necklace. Not gaudy or ostentatious, it was exquisite in its simplicity.

"How beautiful!" Lizzie exclaimed.

"It belonged to my mother," Charles replied, as he lifted the necklace by its chain and stood behind Lizzie to place it around her neck. As he fastened the clasp, his hands lingered on her shoulders, and she closed her eyes, lost in the moment.

When another couple strolled past them, Lizzie turned toward Charles. "I wish I had known her."

Charles became pensive, then replied softly, "She was a Creole you know. White, but born and raised in Nevis. When she moved to England, she tried so hard but ... she never really felt accepted into the inner circle of fashionable society."

"I know a bit of what that is like ..." Lizzie replied quietly.

They stood in a comfortable silence, shrouded in memories. And then, unexpectedly, Charles continued, "I talked to your father."

Lizzie looked at him anxiously. "You did? And did you ask ...?"

"Yes. It was not an easy conversation. But in the end, he said yes!"

Charles reached for her hand, anticipating her excitement. But she could not meet his eyes. "What is it Lizzie? I thought you would be happy!"

Lizzie sat down on a nearby bench, trying to subdue her chaotic emotions. Her fingers fidgeted with the necklace, and she remained silent while Charles paced slowly nearby. When she was finally able to speak, her voice was listless and barely audible. "I tried to tell him about ... your business. I really did. But every time ... it did not seem ... right ..."

"You did not tell him?"

"His health has been so poor. And he has so much on his mind ..."

"So, he agreed to our marriage without knowing ... everything?"

"I thought ... I hoped ..."

Sitting down on the bench beside her, Charles turned her face toward him. "I don't want to delay. I want to set a date for the wedding."

"But I am not ... I cannot ..."

Cutting through her confusion, Charles declared, "I want you to be my wife, and your father gave his consent. Why delay?"

Lizzie stared at Charles uncertainly, then stood up and turned away. She was being unfair to her father. It was impossible! She was fooling herself! So why did she allow herself this flicker of hope at his words? "I don't know if I ..."

"You know this is what you want," he urged gently. "We can be happy together."

"I'm not sure if I ..."

When he placed his hand on her arm, her resolve faltered. As his gaze held hers, something shifted in her, and she knew he could sense it. And when he pulled her against him, she did not resist his embrace.

* * *

Lizzie was subdued when they went back into the ballroom. Charles greeted a few acquaintances, and stopped to chat with some friends, but Lizzie was distracted and ready to go home.

And then, out of the corner of her eye, she noticed a familiar figure striding toward her, a deep frown on his face. Robert! Her brother. She had seen him at home earlier in the day. Why was he here?

"Robert! I did not expect ..."

"Our carriage is out front," he interrupted, as he took her by the arm.

"Don't embarrass me!" Lizzie retorted, jerking her arm away.

"What do you think you are doing to us! To Father!"

Lizzie stared back at Robert, but he was glaring at Charles.

Aware of the curious faces of other guests whispering nearby, Charles turned and led them to a small parlour, where they could talk in private. When the door was closed Robert confronted Charles, his face pale with fury. "Your attentions toward Lizzie are not welcome!"

"She is a grown woman," Charles countered.

"What business is it of yours Robert?" Lizzie challenged her brother.

"I barely recognize you! Allowing Alison Marshall to aid in your deception!"

"What is wrong with an afternoon at the art gallery, or an evening at the theatre?"

"Neglecting your charitable work!"

"It was only a few times."

"Father will never approve!"

"He already has!"

"He would never agree!" Robert snapped.

"I talked to him this morning and he gave his consent," Charles insisted.

Robert searched Lizzie's face, and when she could not meet his gaze he challenged, "You have not told Father the truth!"

Subdued by Robert's accusation, Lizzie was silent as the two men continued to argue about her as if she were not in the room.

"Our father would never have considered your offer if you had been honest with him!" Robert challenged, stepping closer to Charles with fists clenched.

"My intentions are honourable!"

"What do you know of honour?"

"I happen to …"

"I was told that your friends dared you to meet Lizzie!" Robert accused.

Shocked by Robert's allegation, Lizzie stared at Charles, weighing his reply. "It's not like that!"

"Then why …?" Robert asked.

"I love her!"

Lizzie's face flushed as her eyes met Charles', but Robert's retort was contemptuous. "Then you had better give up your business!"

"I have family responsibilities. Employees who depend on me …"

"Employees? Is that what you call them?" Robert challenged.

"Bristol's prosperity depends on businesses such as mine!"

"You're a fool even to consider such a match!" Robert exploded, as he turned and walked angrily out the door. "Lizzie, the carriage is waiting!"

Lizzie looked at Charles standing near the fire, the strain in his face accentuated by the flickering shadows. She hated to leave without resolving things but feared that further delay would only fuel Robert's anger. And her own feelings about Charles were a jumbled mix of guilt and longing. She needed time to think.

"Charles, I must go," she said, her voice distant as she walked toward the door.

"Will I see you tomorrow?" he asked, the uncertainly clear in his face.

She stared back at him, and after a moment's hesitation replied, "Yes, tomorrow."

Chapter 5

The ride home was disagreeable and tense. After exchanging more angry words, Robert and Lizzie each retreated to their own side of the carriage and settled into an uneasy silence.

If only Sam were home, Lizzie mused. *He would understand how I feel. And Robert might listen to him.* But her favourite brother was in his final term at Oxford. And their youngest brother Henry was also busy with his studies.

When the driver pulled up in front of the house, Lizzie rushed up the stairs, hoping to shut herself in her room before Robert could stir up further conflict. When she entered the foyer, she could hear animated conversation in the drawing room. She tiptoed quietly to the staircase and was part-way up when she was startled by her mother's voice. "Lizzie, would you like to join us for tea?"

"Not now Mother," Lizzie snapped, as she continued up the stairs.

"What is the matter? Are you ill?"

When Lizzie glanced back, the concern in her mother's face triggered her tears.

"No ... It's ... It's ..."

And then Robert arrived, forcing the confrontation that she had so long avoided.

"Robert, what is it?" their mother asked anxiously.

"Tell her Lizzie! Or shall I?" Robert challenged.

Lizzie glared at her brother, and when she did not reply, he continued, "I have disturbing news."

"What news?"

"Lizzie is engaged! To a man who … He's … You would never approve."

When their father emerged from the drawing room, Robert asked angrily, "Father, did you know about this engagement?"

"Yes," he nodded. I gave my consent this morning. Lizzie told me he is a fine young man, and that he truly loves her."

"And did she tell you about his business? How he would support her?"

As Robert revealed her secret, Lizzie sat down on the stair and buried her face in her hands.

"He is a … a … slave-owner! His family owns plantations in Nevis!"

"Is this true, Lizzie?" her father exclaimed.

When Lizzie nodded awkwardly, her father sank onto a chair, his face furrowed with distress.

"Lizzie, how could you?" her mother interjected.

Stomach queasy, Lizzie walked uncertainly down the stairs and across the foyer and sank onto her knees before her father. "I'm sorry Father," she pleaded. "I never meant to hurt you."

"When were you planning to tell me?"

Her reply was hesitant, barely audible. "I was waiting for the right time."

"The right time?" he objected. "I have devoted over thirty-five years to fighting slavery!"

The anguish in his words hit their mark, and Lizzie was silent. She had no response. No defense. No excuse. But then Robert's voice intruded on her remorse, his tone like a demanding schoolmaster reprimanding an unruly student. "Imagine the headlines! Famous Abolitionist's daughter marries slave-owner!"

And in an instant her regret was infused with anger, as she stood and turned to face her brother. "You are too concerned with our family's reputation!"

Suddenly, Lizzie was startled when she noticed Tom, standing behind Robert, and blushed at the troubled expression on his face. But Robert, unaware of the exchange, continued his tirade. "What could you have in common?"

"You would not understand!" Lizzie retorted.

"He is very wealthy," he prodded.

Infuriated, Lizzie flared, "That has nothing to do with it!" And before her brother could continue his interrogation, she turned and ran up the stairs, ignoring the clambering voices that attempted to pull her back into the fray. Reaching her room, she slammed the door and stood, trembling, trying to catch her breath.

Agitated voices drifted up the stairs, and she could hear Uncle James' furious brogue above the rest. "How could you Wilber! Such a marriage would be a severe blow to Emancipation!"

And her father's voice, filled with regret and self-reproach. "I trusted her. She has never lied to me before. And she has been so lonely ..."

Lizzie roughly untied her cloak and let it fall to the floor, then threw herself tearfully onto the bed. There was a knock on the door followed by her mother's insistent entreaty, "Lizzie, please join us! We need to talk!" But she just turned her face away and did not reply.

Chapter 6

The tavern was crowded and dimly lit, with the stench of unwashed bodies mingling with a blend of unsavoury odours from the kitchen. Charles glanced anxiously at a pair of shifty-looking men who were watching him intently. *Why does Stuart choose such working-class dives?* Charles grumbled, as he pushed his way past a scrawny man with rotting teeth and putrid breath. *And what was so urgent that he insisted on meeting tonight?* Charles resented the chaos that Stuart created in his life and felt acutely the need to protect his firm's reputation. Yet, this evening the message from Stuart had almost been a relief, since Charles needed an outlet for the turmoil that had been triggered by his confrontation with Robert Wilberforce.

Stuart had chosen a table at the far end of the room, where he could observe the other patrons. When Charles approached, his stomach clenched at the predatory sensuality on Stuart's face, his gaze fixed on a beautiful – and very young – red-haired serving girl near the counter. Pushing aside his revulsion, Charles sat down beside Stuart, his body tense with frustration.

"You look upset, Charles," Stuart commented sardonically, as he poured him a glass of rum from a bottle on the table. "How was the ball with Miss Wilberforce?"

"Her brother Robert made a dramatic entrance," Charles retorted, sipping the amber liquid moodily.

"I told you it wouldn't work," Stuart goaded. Then, with a theatrical gesture, he motioned across the room toward the young serving girl. "Over there. The red-haired wench serving at the bar. She's your type!"

As Charles glanced toward the girl, her cheeks flamed when she caught their eyes upon her.

"A little young, even for you," Charles commented.

"Hmm. With no bad habits," Stuart replied with an insolent smile, as he signaled the girl to bring them a new bottle. Her hand shook slightly as she poured their drinks, her eyes fixed on the glasses. But when she turned to leave, Stuart caught her by the arm and coaxed, "What is your name?"

"Rebecca, Sir," she replied, without meeting his gaze, her voice a strained whisper.

"Look at her Charles," Stuart taunted brazenly. "I'll wager she would soon help you forget the Abolitionist's daughter!"

Charles recognized the challenge in Stuart's eyes, and his spine stiffened with an overwhelming urge to obliterate his arrogant smirk and perhaps, in some small way, to stand up for the honour of the naïve girl who stood humiliated before them. But Stuart's personal life was not Charles' concern unless it affected his work, and so he merely replied, "My taste in women seems to have changed."

Stuart stared provocatively at Charles as he leaned over and whispered in Rebecca's ear. Her body tensed in shock before she turned and walked quickly away, while Charles remained silent, his eyes fixed on his empty glass.

"Perhaps you need some distraction from this ill-fated infatuation," Stuart suggested, as he refilled Charles' glass. "Poker? Or the opera?"

"Stay out of my business, Stuart," Charles snapped, "and tell me what was so urgent that it couldn't wait till a more reasonable time!"

Suddenly, a harsh voice from behind startled Stuart. "You're a hard one to find, Knight!"

The man towered over him – with a deep scar on his cheek and a crooked nose that accentuated his toughness.

"Smithson!" Stuart exclaimed. "I didn't ..."

"No excuses! I want the money you owe me!"

"I don't ... It's not here ..."

"No more delays!" Smithson growled, as he grabbed Stuart's collar and tried to pull him from the chair.

"Get your filthy hands off me!" Stuart shouted, as he jumped to his feet and pushed Smithson's arm away. The two men stared at each other angrily, the veil briefly lifted from Stuart's impudent cynicism to reveal the seething bitterness beneath. But before they could come to blows, Charles stood calmly between them and faced Smithson. "There now, Smithson. No dramatics!" he challenged. "How much does he owe you?"

"Five guineas."

Charles frowned at Stuart, then tossed the coins on the table. After grabbing the money, Smithson glared at Stuart, then stalked toward the exit.

"Your urgent business!" Charles mocked, gratified to see Stuart on the defensive. "Do you know every debt-collector in town?"

Stuart's face betrayed a flash of resentment, but his cynical smile quickly returned as he replied, "I've learned how the game is played. And I so value the generosity of friends like you!"

Charles let the impertinent claim to friendship pass, until Stuart added, "And it is as a friend that I must tell you that I have heard rumours that Miss Wilberforce's father has financial problems of his own."

"It is not a secret that most of his fortune is gone. He was more generous than wise with his money."

"And there is the small detail of how you have made your own fortune ..."

"Stay out of it Stuart!"

Shaking his head in mock sympathy, Stuart exclaimed, "I must in all honesty return to my original suggestion."

"What was that?"

"The redhead of course!" Stuart goaded, nodding towards Rebecca, who was behind the bar serving a customer.

Charles could barely contain his anger, and replied with bitter sarcasm, "Do not offer so casually what you crave for yourself!"

"I am duly rebuked," Stuart sneered. "But the needs of my friends always come first!"

"You're welcome to her!" Charles retorted, shaking with rage – and a crushing need to escape the ghastly place. Without another word he sprang to his feet and forced his way along the narrow aisle between the crowded tables. Near the door, he accidentally bumped into a fierce-looking man, who swore at him belligerently. And then, in a moment which he quickly regretted, he turned around and caught sight of Stuart as he approached the burly bartender and gestured toward Rebecca. Frozen in place, Charles stared at the poor girl with a choking sense of dread as she stood between the two men, eyes downcast, her body tense with fear. When she shook her head, the bartender slapped her on the shoulder – making sure he did not mar her beautiful face – and pushed her toward Stuart, who grasped her triumphantly by the arm. Nauseated with disgust, Charles turned away, forced his way to the door, and escaped into the night. A gentle spring rain had started, and he lifted his face toward the sky, in a vain attempt to cleanse himself from a sickening sense of shame.

* * *

It took several minutes to hail a carriage, and by the time Charles arrived home, he was damp and chilled to the bone. The fire in the marble fireplace of his home office had long since burned out, which only added to his dismal mood, but he did not bother to ring for a servant. The room was shrouded in darkness, apart from a few dim shafts of light which filtered through a large window at one end.

After lighting a few candles, and a lantern on the sideboard, Charles poured himself a glass of whisky from a crystal decanter and stretched out on a brocade settee. As he tried to calm his unruly thoughts, his eyes were drawn to a large portrait of his parents on the opposite wall. A deep sense of loneliness washed over him when he looked at his mother's face – a vulnerable naivety clear in her gentle eyes. And his father towering over her – with a protective hand on her shoulder – comfortable in his privilege and prestige.

He owed so much to his father and felt deeply the responsibility of living up to the trust that he had placed in him when his older brother John had shown no aptitude for business. Yet the evening had left him unsettled, with nagging doubts about the role that a man like Stuart played in managing his plantations.

As he sipped his drink, he pulled one of his father's journals from a shelf. He had kept meticulous records, and as Charles read through it, he was reminded of his father's high standards in the treatment of his employees, and of his philanthropic ventures. He had often said that most plantation owners and managers were greedy and quarrelsome, keeping only a minimum number of slaves who were underfed and overworked – with a high death rate. He had soon realized it was simply good business to keep enough slaves, and to provide them with garden plots to grow their own provisions, since he would get more work from healthy slaves.

Skipping over several unpleasantly graphic entries, Charles found the one he was seeking. "Surely God ordained them for the use and benefit of us: otherwise his Divine Will would surely have been made manifest by some particular Sign or Token." As always, he found his father's pragmatic wisdom very reassuring.

When a small voice reminded him that he had never actually been to Nevis to inspect the plantation himself, he pushed it aside with the assurance that his father had spent much time there. Apart from an occasional need to punish disobedient slaves, and that one unfortunate incident with the sale of Mountravers to Edward Huggins, who proved to be vicious and cruel to his slaves, Charles was confident that with Vincent Bartley in charge, all his properties were managed not only efficiently, but humanely.

Chapter 7

Russell Plantation, Nevis, April 1827

The evening was cool and fresh – Tamar's favourite time of day. It was harvest season, and she was exhausted after wielding a machete to cut sugar cane from dawn to dusk under the blazing sun. But Joseph's job in the intolerable heat of the boiling house, where the cane was turned into molasses, was even worse. His shifts often longer. And when he was assigned to work in the sugar mill, he faced the added risks of injury from the machinery. Although sometimes he had to work through the night, Tamar was thankful that he was home with them tonight.

Impatient to play with his friends, Micah gulped down his rice and beans, and ran off clutching an old ball made of rags. Tamar loved to watch their games, and dreaded the next planting season, when her son would be old enough to join other small children and elderly slaves in the fields.

Crouched on a low stool beside their hut, Joseph was almost finished whittling a toy horse for his son from a scrap of wood. Tamar put a kettle of water on the fire, then sat down on the packed earth in front of her husband and leaned back against his legs. Setting aside his carving, Joseph gently massaged the stress of the day from the tense muscles in her neck and shoulders. She melted into him, always amazed that such powerful, calloused hands could be so sensitive when they touched her skin.

She treasured this familiar routine. The quiet voices of her friends chatting around their fires. Cheerful strains of old Ben's harmonica drifting across the square. And the children – especially the children – shouting, bickering, and laughing. So full of life!

But suddenly the peaceful moment was shattered by the sound of strident voices cursing loudly, coming from the direction of the lane to the Big House. Unexpectedly their Overseer, Jackson, strode into the square, and asked, almost reluctantly, "Anyone seen Levi?"

When the slaves milling in the square denied seeing him, Jackson became agitated, which was unusual for a man who was known for his fairness and even temper. "Someone must have seen him! Master Russell gave orders ..."

"What's taken' ye' so long, Jackson?" shouted a huge, burly stranger with an unruly red beard who erupted into the square. "We ain't got all night!" He was followed by a tall, sinewy man who Tamar named "Fox" due to his sharp nose and beady eyes.

Waving a pair of manacles above his head, Fox threatened the slaves, "Give us Levi, unless you want to take his place!"

Barely able to breathe, Tamar, like the others, stared at the ground, avoiding eye contact with the men. She wondered why they wanted Levi. He was a good boy who never gave any trouble. But then an alarming thought came to her. Although he was not yet an adult, he was tall and strong. And he was an orphan.

The frightened voice of Micah burst into her thoughts. "Mama! Mama!" When she looked up, he was in the middle of the square, running toward her. "Ah, we got a volunteer!" shouted Fox with a vicious smirk, as he grabbed Micah, and lifted him above his head. "Do ye want te take Levi's place, boy?"

When she saw Joseph take a step forward, Tamar was terrified that his muscular frame would antagonize the men. And so, with a hand on his arm, she pushed him back, and stepped into the square. "Leave him be!" she implored, barely able to mask her anger.

"What have we here?" leered Fox, ogling Tamar from head to toe. "This one would fetch a much better price than a young buck like Levi!"

In an instant, a barrage of unwelcome images flashed through Tamar's mind. A tall man on a horse, staring at her in a way that made her sick inside. The strange look on Massa Russell's face when the stranger laughed about his debt. And the way he had walked away without saying a word.

But then, there was a scuffle at the far side of the square, and Red-Beard emerged, dragging Levi by a chain attached to manacles on his wrists.

"You can have this one back for now," sneered his partner, as he dropped Micah into Tamar's arms. "But you never know when we'll be back!"

Tamar stroked Micah's hair lovingly as he clung to her, and she soon felt Joseph's strong arms around them both. But her relief was tinged with sadness at the fate of poor Levi. And as much as she tried to push aside her fears, she could not forget the chilling words, "you never know when we'll be back!"

Chapter 8

Oh no! Lizzie moaned, as the grandfather clock in the foyer struck 9:00. *I've overslept!*

Throwing back her blankets, she rushed across the room to the oak wardrobe, and flung open the doors. *What shall I wear?* she fretted, as she looked through the limited selection of morning dresses – most a couple of seasons out of date. Then a lavender gown caught her eye – the perfect choice. She dressed hurriedly, fumbling to do up the buttons and sash in back. When she turned toward the mirror, she noticed that she had not removed her brooch the last time she wore the dress. Frowning slightly, she ran her finger over the embossed image - a reminder of her vow. But then her eyes were drawn to her dressing table, where the early morning light sparkled on the beautiful sapphire necklace. As she fastened it around her neck, she studied her reflection in a full-length mirror – impatient to see Charles, and the look in his eyes.

And so, setting aside her misgivings, Lizzie pried open the latch of the brooch, pulled it from the fabric and placed it on the dressing table. Then, after a moment of indecision, she picked it up and put it out of sight in the top drawer. After styling her hair, she wrapped a long white silk shawl around her shoulders, adding a decorative flourish that concealed the necklace.

When she looked out her window, Lizzie was relieved that the back garden was deserted. She opened the door and peered cautiously into the hallway before walking on tiptoe to the back staircase. Halfway down, she froze when one of the stairs creaked, but all she could hear was the voice of Mrs. Knowles in the kitchen giving instructions to Phoebe, the cook. "Fry it till it's crisp."

Relieved that they had not heard her, Lizzie darted down the stairs and past the open kitchen door without being seen. But when she began to open the back door to the garden, the hinge creaked loudly. Mrs. Knowles poked her head out and declared in a no-nonsense voice, "Your father said to ask you to join them for breakfast in the dining room."

Lizzie was tempted to continue her escape but knew she could not avoid facing them indefinitely. And so, with a sigh of resignation, she closed the door and walked down the hall to the dining room, where the appetizing smell of bacon, eggs and hot buttered scones reminded her how hungry she was.

Uncle James was in the midst of telling a humorous story, no doubt attempting – without success – to lighten the gloomy mood. When Lizzie entered, there was an awkward moment of silence, until Robert motioned toward her empty chair, and commented sarcastically, "So good of you to join us, Lizzie. The food was getting cold, so we started without you."

Ignoring him, Lizzie took her place, keenly aware of Tom's troubled gaze. She had always valued his opinion and hated to disappoint him. Her father was pushing uneaten food around his plate, and her mother fidgeted nervously – clearly close to tears. But her brother William, unfazed by the tension in the room, passed her a dish of eggs and teased, "I must say, Lizzie, I owe you a debt of gratitude!"

"Gratitude?"

"This current – situation," he quipped. "As you know, I have made my share of, shall we say, questionable decisions, in the past. So, I will gladly give over the title of black sheep!"

"Your frivolity is not helpful!" Robert retorted.

"I beg to differ, dear brother," William smirked. "What are your thoughts on the matter, Uncle James?"

His hot temper seemed to have cooled somewhat, and with his usual blunt wit, her uncle coaxed, "Ach, Lass, I know how ye feel. When Romance beckons, Reason is oft forsaken – a drab spinster on the edge of a dance floor!"

"I've forsaken Reason for purposes other than Romance!" William laughed, causing his wife Mary to stare at him with a slight frown.

"Does this situation amuse you?" Robert replied angrily. Then, turning to Lizzie, he challenged, "You must see that this – alliance – is untenable. Do you not have the common courtesy to discuss ..."

Unexpectedly, their father stood up and silenced Robert. "I will talk to Lizzie." When her mother began to rise from her chair, he put a kind hand on her shoulder and said firmly, "Alone!"

When Lizzie joined her father in the parlour, he was staring out the window, his face creased with anguish. His hair was disheveled, and his suit was wrinkled, and when Lizzie noticed wilting flowers in two of his buttonholes, she unconsciously fell back into a ritual that was familiar to them both. Plucking a fresh flower from a vase on the table, Lizzie tenderly removed the faded blooms from her father's buttonholes and replaced them with the fresh one. She tidied his hair with an affectionate smile, then met his gaze uncertainly. "I never intended ..."

"I thought you understood," he said sadly. "It was not just a career!"

"I know."

"The plight of the slaves ... their cry for justice ... are as much a part of me as ..." He shook his head in frustration. There were no words.

"Charles has not asked me to go to Nevis. He conducts all his business in Bristol."

"Would distance diminish your complicity?"

Stung by the truth of his question, Lizzie became defensive. "Robert assumes I would fall in love with a complete rogue, but Charles is not like that."

"But ... a slave-owner ..."

"He runs his plantations with high standards ..."

Her father looked at her sharply, then pressed further. "How can he be sure? Being a plantation owner from a distance is often worse since the overseers lack accountability."

Lizzie looked away, at a loss for words.

"Robert had other concerns."

"What did he tell you?"

"Charles' business provides mortgages for other plantation owners to expand their holdings ..."

"But if you only knew him ..."

"He is a very wealthy man ..."

"How can you judge him?" Lizzie protested. "You lived for wealth and prestige in your youth!"

"Yes. I wasted so much time – and money – on shallow diversions ..."

"You of all people know he can change," Lizzie pleaded. "What if this is his chance?"

Then, unexpectedly, Robert, who had entered the room unnoticed, interrupted, "You think you can reform him?"

"Robert, don't interfere," their father chided.

Furious at her brother, Lizzie added, "This is a private conversation!"

But, unable to restrain himself, Robert continued, "You're fooling yourself!"

"Who could live up to your standards?" Lizzie taunted.

"I did not determine them ..."

"With your Oxford education. Your double firsts ..."

"Are you harbouring old jealousies?"

"No, but you are a man! What choices do I ..."

Towering over her with clenched fists, Robert shouted, "You can choose to do what is right!"

Speechless with rage, Lizzie stared at her brother, then began to walk toward the door. "I have to meet Charles."

"Are you going to see him in public?" Robert challenged.

"I will take Ann as a chaperone," Lizzie retorted. Ann had been a hardworking parlour maid when she was younger and had only been kept on because Lizzie's father was too soft-hearted to dismiss elderly and infirm servants when they could no longer perform their duties. *I'm sure she will enjoy sitting on a bench under a shady tree,* Lizzie thought, which would give her time alone with Charles.

Turning to his father, Robert exclaimed, "You can't let her go!"

As Lizzie walked out the door into the hallway, she felt a sense of satisfaction at her brother's frustration, but it was quickly tainted with regret when her father replied sadly, "What would you have me do? Lock her in her room?"

Chapter 9

It was a beautiful spring day – warm enough that Lizzie had left her shawl in the carriage. The park was crowded with couples strolling arm in arm through the ornamental gardens, and children playing under the watchful supervision of their guardians. A variety of boats passed by on the river, as ducks and swans swam near the bank.

But despite the tranquil scene, Lizzie's emotions were in turmoil. And the romantic stroll that she had envisioned had quickly turned into a heated argument.

"I don't understand why you cannot sell your plantations," she exclaimed, turning toward Charles in frustration.

"I've already told you …"

"There are so many other worthy ventures for investment. Why not join the fight against slavery?"

"I am not in any position to change things."

"Uncle James gave up a successful law practice in St. Kitt's for Abolition," Lizzie responded scornfully.

"The poor in England are often worse off than slaves in the West Indies!" Charles retorted.

"The presence of one injustice does not excuse us from fighting another!"

"You've been cloistered too long in a world of noble causes!"

"My father's achievements are very real!"

And then, breaching her defenses, Charles challenged, "And will you change the world as he has?"

His barb cut deep, piercing her self-righteousness, and exposing her insecurities. Speechless and angry, she stared at him in dismay. And then, overcome by shame, and a need to escape his scrutiny, she turned away and began to walk quickly along a narrow path that branched off the well-travelled walkway they were on.

When Lizzie looked back, Charles was following a few steps behind – his longer stride easily matching hers. She increased her pace, driven on by a chaotic jumble of distress, regret and confusion. Unexpectedly, the path began to lead up a hill toward the ruins of an old tower. Unwilling to swallow her pride, Lizzie continued up the rocky terrain, and had to stop several times along the way to catch her breath. And although she refused to talk to Charles, she was far too aware of his presence behind her – and of the relief that surged through her every time she saw that he had not turned back.

As they rested for a final time near the top of the hill, Charles approached Lizzie and put his hand gently on her arm. "You can't escape reality," he entreated.

"Reality?"

"Lofty ideals may stir the imagination, but real choices are made for more practical reasons."

"Like building your empire?"

"Or because you love someone!"

"You said it yourself. We must face reality ..."

"Lizzie ..."

Fighting back tears, she whispered, "Our differences are too great."

Then, before he could reply, she turned away, and continued up the path. When she stumbled slightly, Charles offered his hand, but she refused to take it, and continued stubbornly on her own until, breathless and flushed from exertion, she reached the top of the hill.

Only two walls of the ruined tower were intact and formed part of a turret – the sole part of the roof still standing. The other two walls had been destroyed above waist level, and one contained a doorway, which Lizzie entered cautiously, careful to avoid the piles of rubble inside the entrance.

She crossed to the gaping hole in the adjoining wall and was captivated by the panorama below. Sunlight reflected from the river, which was dotted with tiny boats as it meandered through a patchwork of grassy fields – with a glimpse of the sea far in the distance. The people in the park looked like miniature dolls, arrayed in a rainbow of bright colours. And when she squinted her eyes against the glare of the sun, she thought she could see Ann with her yellow parasol – no doubt impatient for her return.

Lizzie sensed Charles' presence behind her, and they stood in silence for several moments. But when he moved closer, his breath warm on her neck, she protested, "No!" and pulled away to face him.

"You cannot deny your feelings!" he exclaimed.

"I am too old for fairy tales ..."

"I saw it in your eyes ..."

"... and happy ever after endings!"

Charles looked like he would argue with her, but then Lizzie noticed the hint of a smile around his mouth. And she knew that her face was sending a message that belied her words.

"And yet you've led me here ..." he challenged gently, as he took a step toward her and stood between her and the doorway behind him.

Lizzie blushed as she stared at him, wide-eyed with longing. "Charles, I ..."

"A secluded tower ..." he continued playfully.

"It is getting late ..."

Placing a gentle finger across Lizzie's lips, he teased, "... with no escape!"

When he kissed her tentatively on the cheek, Lizzie breathed, "Ann will wonder ..." But she did not push him away, even when he kissed her gently on the lips.

As his kisses became more passionate, her body came alive with sensations that she had never felt before. Her feeble attempts at resistance fell away as she yielded to the desire that he awakened in her. And in that moment, as her heart won out over her head, nothing else seemed to matter.

* * *

As the driver helped Lizzie down from the carriage, she hoped that her family would still be eating dinner, and that she could sneak up to her room without being seen. But the scent of lilacs filled the air, and the rosy glow of the sunset tinted the daffodils and tulips along the garden path with such vivid hues that she closed her eyes and lingered there, aching to feel Charles' arms around her again, his breath warm on her neck, her lips on fire from his caresses.

An abrupt movement on the other side of the small garden jolted her back to reality as she discovered that she was not alone. She froze awkwardly when she realized that Tom was sitting on a bench, a book closed beside him, and had most likely been watching her the whole time.

"Tom! I ..." Lizzie stuttered, at a loss for words.

His expression was guarded – unreadable - as he replied quietly, "I never expected ..."

Suddenly aware that Tom was staring at her necklace, Lizzie tried to divert his attention, while she adjusted her shawl. "I did not mean to miss dinner. It took some time to hail a carriage."

After an uncomfortable silence, Tom suggested, "Would you like to go for a stroll?"

"It is getting late," she declined. "Perhaps tomorrow."

A frown briefly creased his face, before he replied softly, "Yes. Tomorrow."

Anxious to end their awkward encounter, Lizzie began to walk quickly along the path toward the rear of the house. She could hear the cheerful shouts of her nephew, William, from the other side of the garden, where a swing had been suspended from an old oak tree. "Grandpa, push me again. I want to go up high!" On another evening she might have joined them, since her father's childlike spirit, and love of children, were contagious.

She had reached the middle of the tiny kitchen garden when a familiar, sharp-tongued voice from behind compelled her to turn around. Mrs. Knowles was limping along the path carrying a basket of freshly picked vegetables. "You ought to be ashamed, Miss Lizzie!" she scolded. "Chasin' him 'cross the country on your own!"

"Robert talks too much!" Lizzie snapped.

Setting the basket on the ground, Mrs. Knowles raised a gnarled finger and chided, "He'll not be the only one!"

"I'm a grown woman!"

"You're behav'in like a child!"

"In my friends' houses, the servants don't talk back like Father allows you to!" Lizzie replied defiantly.

"In your friends' houses, daughters don't deceive their fathers about who they want to marry!"

"I thought you understood …" Lizzie pleaded.

"I understand that many a young woman chases after a handsome face and a flatterin' tongue but wakes up beside a stranger who turns her life into a nightmare!"

Shocked by words that she did not fully understand, Lizzie did not know what to say. And then the old woman, who had served their family loyally for so many years, continued more gently. "Master Wilberforce is far too kind-hearted for his own good, Lizzie. I never knew a man like him for kindness to everyone, rich or poor."

"I know, but Charles is not …"

"Perhaps he should have been firmer with all of you. Master William's debts have been a burden …."

"Yes, but why won't anyone give Charles a chance?"

"Miss Lizzie, you can make as many excuses as you want, but your father doesn't deserve such treatment!"

Agitated and confused, Lizzie turned away and stalked toward the house.

Chapter 10

The inkpot was empty. Frustrated that she could not finish her letter, Lizzie looked through the drawers of her desk without success. She had managed to reach her bedroom without any more family encounters. Did she dare go to the library in search of ink?

The hallway was quiet, and she could hear animated conversation drifting up from the drawing room downstairs. Relieved that the way was clear, she walked furtively to the library at the end of the hall, quietly opened the door, and closed it silently behind her.

The room was in shadow, dimly lit by the waning rays of the sunset, with a fire flickering in the fireplace. And so, Lizzie did not realize that she was not alone until she was startled with the faint sound of singing coming from the other end of the room. The voice wavering slightly with age, but still beautiful. The single-handed piano accompaniment halting, and awkward. The hymn so familiar. Amazing Grace.

Before she could turn around, her father called her name, and she reluctantly walked over to the piano. He made room for her on the bench, and she took over playing fluently, as their voices blended for the next verse.

"Singing that hymn always gives me hope," he said.

Pierced by the pain in her father's voice she replied, "I know how you love it."

"If John Newton's wretched life could be transformed from slave-ship

45

captain to Abolitionist ..." His reply remained unfinished, suspended in the air between them. But Lizzie had grown up with this story. It was part of the fabric of her life.

Walking over to the fire, Lizzie stirred it with a poker, then sat on a nearby stool. Her father joined her, choosing a chair that he found comfortable for his pain-ridden spine. Both seemed lost in their own thoughts as they watched the flickering flames in companionable silence for several minutes.

The sound of running footsteps was followed by William Junior's excited voice. "Uncle James, can you read me a story?"

"Which one do you want to hear?" Uncle James replied.

"The one about the pirates!"

Lizzie and her father exchanged a smile. Then, as she poked at the fire again, she mused, "The fire tells so many stories."

"A chaotic duel between light and shadow."

Gripped by a memory, Lizzie continued, "Amelia Cox used to look in the flames and see herself as a princess rescued by a valiant knight, but I ... I was a heroine who would slay the dragons of injustice."

"Like Lady Middleton?"

Jolted by the reminder, Lizzie stared at her father before nodding reluctantly, "I always admired her."

With a gentle smile, her father added, "She was not deterred by my excuses. When she introduced me to James Ramsay, and I heard for myself about slavery ..."

"I wanted to be like her," Lizzie admitted sadly. "A woman in a man's world, exerting a quiet influence behind the scenes ... But now ..."

With a gesture of resignation, she stood up, and walked over to a large candelabra on a nearby desk. As she lit the candles, she grasped for words that would convey her struggle. "Like Viola in Twelfth Night, disguising herself as a man ... I dressed in borrowed garments."

"Borrowed?" her father inquired.

"I was the Liberator's daughter," Lizzie shrugged. "Clothed in your reputation, I never doubted my zeal."

"Do you regret the way you were raised?" he asked, his voice husky with pain.

"There came a time when Viola had reason to end her charade ..."

"Her love for Orsino."

Lizzie nodded, then walked over to a bookcase, to retrieve her copy of Twelfth Night. Flipping through it, she found the passage she was looking for and read it aloud slowly:

"Poor lady, she were better love a dream,

Disguise, I see thou art a wickedness.

How easy is it for the proper false

In women's waxen hearts to set their forms!

Alas, our frailty is the cause, not we,

For such as we are made of, such we be."

"In my youth, my life was a pathetic clamour for pleasure and approval," her father countered. "Nothing to be proud of."

"But after your conversion ..."

"Many of my friends and colleagues who attended church on Sundays thought that Christian faith had no relevance for the rest of the week. When I began to believe that Christ's challenge to love others as we love ourselves applies to people who are very different from us - including slaves on the other side of the ocean – they laughed at me and called me a fanatic. I would have quit politics if not for John Newton's encouragement. And even later at Clapham with the support of Henry and James and Zachary and Thomas Clarkson and the others, the name 'Clapham Sect' was coined by our opponents as an insult."

Returning the book to the shelf, Lizzie sat down again and pleaded, "Don't you think God asks too much sometimes?"

"It is not always easy ..."

"Do you want me to obey Him out of guilt?"

Her Father's reply was gentle, as he met her eyes with a poignant mixture of love and sadness. "Not at all. But there are still dragons to slay."

Turning away from his scrutiny, she fixed her gaze on the fire as she whispered sadly, "Little girls grow up."

Chapter 11

The book was dull at best, but this evening Charles' distracted thoughts could make no sense of it at all. Agitated and restless, he closed it in disgust and began to pace around the room. When he had been with Lizzie that afternoon, he had allowed the thrill of passion to convince her – and himself – that they could have a future together. A future that he craved with an almost physical hunger. Because, although there had been other women who were more beautiful – more refined – Lizzie had stirred something in him that had taken him by surprise. A dormant sense that despite his wealth, there was something missing. And although the pragmatism that made him so successful in business warned him it was all idealistic nonsense, when he was with her, she had more influence on him than he dared to admit.

He paused in front of an assortment of newspaper cartoons, which had been collected by his father, displayed prominently on a wall of his office. Several lampooned the sugar boycott that had been promoted by the free-produce movement. His father had laughed when he recalled how high-society ladies had stopped using sugar produced by slave labour in their tea. And as he had predicted, they soon lost interest and moved on to the next cause that came into vogue. But Lizzie was not like them. And Lizzie still refused sugar in her tea. Sugar. The "white gold" that fueled his prosperity!

A knock on the office door startled Charles from his reverie. Without waiting for an invitation, his associate, Gerald, walked in followed by his friend Matthew, who Charles had met once or twice before.

"Why are you working so late Charles? Come for a drink with us."

Gesturing toward a pile of folders on his desk Charles replied, "I wish I could, but I am behind on these reports."

"Charles, I recall that your brother John chided you for working too hard!"

"You're right," he smiled. "I cannot concentrate on work now anyway."

They hailed a carriage, and while Gerald and Matthew bantered jovially, Charles drifted into a fitful sleep and did not wake until they clattered to a stop. "Where are we?" he frowned, disoriented by the raucous crowd milling about a narrow lane of squalid tenements.

"Stuart gave us the name of the pub, but the driver says we'll have to walk the rest of the way."

Stuart! Charles fumed. *I should have known. Gerald seems to spend far too much time with him!* He was tempted to turn back, but Gerald had already paid the driver, who wasted no time heading back to a safer part of the city. And so, with no other option, Charles followed Gerald and Matthew as they tried to push their way past the street vendors hawking their wares, and the women of the night whose shabby finery left little to the imagination. But Charles and his companions wore their privilege like a banner draped around their shoulders, and it was impossible for them to blend in. When a gaunt little girl leaning on a cane shoved a chipped bowl in his face, Charles hesitated. Staring uncertainly at the frail creature, he dug in his pocket and tossed a farthing into her bowl. Instantly, he was hemmed in as more beggars surged around him, and he realized he had become separated from the others.

"Move aside!" Matthew shouted, pushing through the crowd. "Hurry, Charles! This way."

After rejoining his friends, Charles grumbled, "I wish Stuart was not drawn to such sleazy places!"

"He seems to crave novel diversions!" Matthew smirked.

"Vulgar would be more accurate," Charles scoffed.

When a pair of prostitutes, garish with cherry red lips and rouged cheeks, beckoned to them, Matthew ogled them good-naturedly, as Gerald called out, "Maybe later."

The appalling scene was like a slap in the face. *What would Lizzie think if she knew I was here?* For an instant Charles considered turning back. But logic soon won out as he reminded himself that it would be much too dangerous to walk alone through the crowd at this late hour.

* * *

When he looked at his cards, Stuart concealed a smile – confident that his luck was changing. The saucy barmaid, Rose, returned frequently to their table to refill their glasses, and to flirt brazenly with Matthew, who could not take his eyes from her. But Stuart's attention was focused on Charles, who was frowning at him from the other side of the table. "We're tired of hearing about it, Stuart," he snapped. "Take your turn!"

Ignoring him, Stuart drained the rum in his glass, relishing the way it loosened his tongue. "I've made a decision, Charles, he quipped. "I'll take you with me!"

Gerald and Matthew exchanged a cynical smile, but Charles did not restrain his irritation. "Don't be an idiot!"

Unfazed by his response, Stuart continued sarcastically, "You were born for plantation life. My cousin Vincent has been a true mentor to me and would teach you so much!"

"Play your hand!"

"Vincent would take you on a tour of the slave quarters," Stuart baited, as he tossed a card onto the table. "Show you the night life!"

"I would never degrade myself ..." Charles retorted, shocked by what Stuart was implying.

Savouring his discomfort, Stuart feigned innocence. "Never? I doubt that, Charles."

"This is getting tedious," Charles replied, but Gerald and Matthew obviously found the dispute highly entertaining.

With a sly smile, Stuart motioned for Rose to bring another bottle of rum. When she had refilled all the glasses, Stuart stood up dramatically. "A toast! To the one true religion in this country!" He paused theatrically, looking directly at each of his companions.

"Well, don't keep us in suspense!" Matthew laughed.

"I have it on the highest authority -," Stuart declared, with a comical bow, "Mr. Charles Pinney himself - that the true religion in this country is business and trade ..."

Gesturing to the money exchanging hands at the gambling tables around them, he continued, "Profit and greed its primary virtues! Poverty and privation its only sins!" Raising his glass with a flourish, Stuart exclaimed, "To our one true religion!"

"To our one true religion!" cheered Gerald, quickly echoed by Matthew.

When Charles, appearing indifferent, did not raise his glass, Stuart gloated inwardly. But Charles was not so easily routed, and his challenge was pointed. "You have long benefited from that religion yourself!"

"No doubt," Stuart mocked. "But I could never match your piety!"

Charles' reply dripped with disdain. "Our friend Smithson seems to have transformed your attitude toward money!"

The animosity that Stuart had been trying to veil with satirical wit flashed to the surface, and he knew it must be visible in his face. But masking it with a scornful smile, he raised his glass once more and taunted, "It is a comfort that you never change!"

Barely restraining his laughter, Gerald shuffled the deck and dealt the cards, as Charles and Stuart sipped their drinks in strained silence.

* * *

It was a dismal place, almost deserted apart from the shadow people who lurked in obscurity under the cover of darkness. Legions of rats swarmed over mounds of refuse, attracted by the vile stench of rotting food and human waste.

At this late hour it was not easy to find a carriage in such a place, and after Matthew followed Rose out the door of the tavern, Charles and Gerald had to depend on Stuart to find their way home.

Charles seethed with frustration when a wrong turn led them deeper into a confusing maze of narrow lanes and alleys, rather than toward the footbridge that would take them to a carriage stop on the other side of the canal. Suddenly, a ragged old man who reeked of whiskey emerged from the gloom and stumbled into their path. Alert for signs of danger, Charles tensed, ready for a fight. But when the broken-down beggar simply held out his torn hat, Charles glanced at him in disgust and gave him a wide berth.

"Look, at the end of the lane," Gerald exclaimed. "I think I can see a boat!"

When they emerged onto the towpath beside the canal, a variety of small boats were illuminated by the light of the full moon. Most of the narrowboats were moored for the night, but a few flyboats sped past, followed by a heavily-laden barge, carrying cargo to the harbour. And within easy walking distance was the footbridge that spanned the canal.

As they walked past an abandoned warehouse, an aging prostitute called out, clearly desperate for a customer. Charles glanced at her briefly, then quickly turned away, repulsed by her wrinkled face and toothless grin. Yet despite their recent detour, Gerald remained in good spirits. Motioning in the direction of the harbour, he confided, "I used to dream of going to sea when I was a boy."

"The reality is less exciting than the dream," Stuart laughed.

"You had an eventful voyage ..." Gerald nodded.

"Eventful ... and long, with a ship full of sailors, and no women to share your bed!"

A shabby vagrant huddled in a shop doorway glanced up at them briefly, then indifferently closed his eyes.

"And when you get home to Nevis?"

"It has it charms!" Stuart smirked.

"What is Vincent like?" Gerald coaxed.

"He has a good head for business, but his real passions lie elsewhere!"

"Does he really visit the slave quarters?"

"He claims they're an inferior species, but he has a special ... appreciation ... for the women."

"Enough Stuart!" Charles interjected. "My father would never have allowed such behaviour!"

"But Charles, when was the last time your father – or you – visited Nevis?"

A cold wave of doubt washed over Charles as he realized the truth of Stuart's assertion.

"And you will recall that rather unpleasant incident a few years back, when your father sold one of his properties to a man who was, shall we say, rather harsh to his slaves," Stuart goaded. "Quite a scandal at the time, what with all the scourging and the branding the man used to control his human property. But fortunately, it all settled down, and the other plantation owners seldom mention it any more."

Some crew members who were playing a game of dice on a barge tied nearby looked up at Stuart suspiciously, then went back to their game.

Desperate to end the conversation, Charles walked ahead of them. He paused briefly on the middle of the footbridge to look at silhouettes of ships in the distance, anticipating once again the day that Stuart would board one of them and return to the plantation life he described so vividly.

Chapter 12

They came just before dawn. Furtive and stealthy. Cloaked in darkness.

The creaking of a rusty hinge pulled Tamar from a restless dream, but it was too late. A shadowy figure loomed in the doorway of the hut, and before she could call out, he grabbed her by both arms and jerked her from the mattress. "We meet again," he hissed, running his hands over her as he pulled her body against his. "I bin thinkin' 'bout ye a lot since last time."

Although she could not see his face, the voice was distinctive, and filled her with disgust. Fox! His tall, lean form bending over her – his sour breath warm on her face.

Overwhelmed by his strength, she closed her eyes, her mind numb with fear. Escape impossible.

Then, unexpectedly, a bulky form came up behind Fox and growled, "Let 'er go, fool! Master Russell's not payin' us to sample his merchandise!" It was Red-Beard's voice.

Fox grumbled in frustration, but reluctantly released Tamar. And then, as the glow of sunlight began to filter through a window, she saw him. Micah, struggling in Red-Beard's arms, the man's huge hand clamped over his mouth. "Behave yerself woman," he warned, "if ye want te see yer brat again!"

And so, although every instinct screamed to pounce on Red-Beard's back and fight for her son, Tamar stood in mute resignation while Fox fastened shackles around her wrists and ankles. As they dragged her from the hut, she looked around the dusty square, wondering what had happened to Joseph. He was working a night shift at the plantation mill, but he should have come home by now.

And then, she saw him, emerging from between two huts on the other side of the square, his arms loaded with firewood despite his obvious exhaustion. As his eyes met hers, rage raw in his face, he dropped the wood and began to run toward them.

"Joseph, no!" she shouted. "We got to be together!"

He stopped in the middle of the square, fists clenched, the tension visible in his powerful arms – barely able to restrain his urge to defend his family. And then, Tamar breathed a sigh of relief when he raised his hands in surrender and stood quietly while Fox roughly chained his wrists and ankles, clearly relishing his humiliation. As tears stung her eyes, Tamar clung to their last hope. Better together than Joseph sold away from her. Or dead. And Massa had always said he would never separate families. They were counting on that promise.

Suddenly, at the sound of the bell, the square filled with bewildered slaves. Although their faces masked their emotions, Tamar could see the fear in their eyes. Her throat tightened when she noticed her friend Elsie, knowing they would likely never meet again.

Despite Joseph's compliance, Fox gleefully prodded him to the wagon with a pointed stick. And taking advantage of Tamar's chains, he picked her up with grasping hands that made her flesh crawl, insisting that she sit beside him on the front bench. Feigning kindness, he allowed Micah to snuggle against her on the other side, although his real motives were no doubt to keep the child quiet.

As they set out on the road, with Red-Beard in the driver's seat, Fox could not keep his hands off Tamar, his eyes triumphant as he glanced over at the unveiled loathing on Joseph's face.

"What did I say about samplin' Master Russell's merchandise!" Red-Beard snapped when he glanced back and saw Fox's hand caressing Tamar's neck.

"I'm not samplin'. Just inspectin," Fox quipped. With an indifferent shrug, Red-Beard turned away and guided the wagon down the road, toward a grim future that filled Tamar with dread.

Chapter 13

The allure was instinctive. Deeply rooted. Even primal. A haven in the midst of turmoil. The scent of the freshly turned soil a healing balm – diverting her thoughts from the tangled muddle of the present to a less complicated time.

Kneeling in a multihued bed of daffodils. hyacinths and tulips in the small garden, Lizzie was startled by Tom's voice behind her. "You've always loved gardening," he smiled, offering a hand to help her up.

"Tom, I ..." she began awkwardly, removing her gloves and trying to brush the dirt from her apron.

"Remember that garden at Clapham?" he reminisced.

"Mrs. Knowles used to scold me for soiling my clothes," Lizzie laughed. "Mother despaired of ever making a lady out of me."

"She needn't have worried," he teased. "Although your interests have always gone beyond frivolous social gatherings and the latest fashions from Paris."

She stared at him, unsure whether there was a hidden challenge behind his words. They were close in age and had grown up together. Sometimes she felt that he could see into her soul – a disconcerting thought in the current context.

As they began to stroll along a winding flagstone path, Lizzie attempted to distract Tom's attention. "I read your essay on Milton. It was brilliant."

But Tom's reply was pointed. "Did you read the previous one in The Edinburgh Review? The one about slavery?"

"Yes. Of course," she replied awkwardly, unable to meet his eyes."

"Lizzie, you have always been as passionate as I have about Emancipation. I don't understand ..."

Lizzie faced him, cringing at the disappointment on his face. Robert's anger only fueled her own, but with Tom it was different. She had always valued his opinion. "It is hard to explain. When I am with Charles, I feel ..." How could she make him understand? Words seemed so inadequate.

"Robert says he is wealthy."

"You know I do not care about that!"

"A man of prestige and influence ..."

Flushed with anger, Lizzie retorted, "Do you think me so shallow?"

Tom started to reply then, with obvious effort, he took a step back, and turned his attention toward a patch of shrubs that had been pruned into a variety of decorative shapes. When he spoke again, his voice was controlled and formal. "Your father does not feel well enough to come to my speech tonight."

"His back gives him more trouble," Lizzie replied, hating the tension between them.

"He said you have invited Charles."

"I was hoping he might hear something ..." Lizzie pleaded.

He turned abruptly toward her, shaking his head in disbelief. "You want me to sway him? What if he never gives up his inheritance?"

"I don't know ..." she replied defensively.

"You don't know?"

As Lizzie stared back at Tom, her vain attempt to make him understand turned to defiance as she shouted back, "Yes. Yes, I will marry him!"

For a few moments Tom's distress was naked in his face. Then, he masked his feelings, and replied, "Pardon me," as if talking to a stranger. "I mistook you for someone I once knew." And turning abruptly, he headed back along the path toward the house. Lizzie watched him anxiously, hoping that he would turn around. But as he continued to walk away without looking back, Lizzie's defiance dissolved in a flood of tears.

* * *

Stevens was a skilled butler, adept at concealing his responses in even the most trying situation. But when Lizzie arrived unannounced, and somewhat disheveled, at Alison Marshall's front door, she detected a flicker of surprise in his serious eyes.

I should have changed and washed my face before coming, she thought, as she passed a mirror and noticed tear-smudged streaks of dirt on her face, and stains where her dress had not been covered by her apron.

When she was shown into the parlour, Lizzie stared sheepishly at the puzzled expression on Alison's face. Then, struck by the absurdity of the situation, the two friends were overcome by contagious laughter, quickly followed by Lizzie's unrestrained tears.

Alison immediately rang for the housekeeper, who ushered Lizzie out of the room with bustling efficiency. When she returned a few minutes later, Lizzie was not only clean, but wearing a lovely peach-coloured spring dress.

As Alison handed her a cup of tea, Lizzie allowed her turbulent emotions to spill over into unfiltered words, knowing that her friend's gentle heart would keep them safe.

"I never meant to hurt Father ..."

Alison hesitated slightly before probing gently, "Lizzie, are you sure ...?"

"You know how I feel ..."

Shaking her head, Alison replied, "I have never been romantic."

There was an awkward silence between them, and Lizzie knew that the topic made her friend uncomfortable. But she had questions that consumed her – that she had never spoken aloud. "Before you were married, did you ever lay awake at night ... and wonder ...?" The expression on her face left no doubt about her meaning. "Did your body come alive ... in new ... ways ...?"

"Lizzie!" Alison exclaimed, her cheeks scarlet.

Frustrated by her friend's refusal to answer, Lizzie persisted, "Does John make you ... happy?"

Alison looked startled, as a myriad of conflicting emotions flitted across her face. For several moments she was silent, the only sound the ticking of the clock on the mantelpiece. But then, as if rousing herself from a dream, Alison stood up and motioned for Lizzie to follow.

After ascending the mahogany staircase that led from the main foyer to the second floor, Alison pushed open the door of the nursery. It was a cheerful room, with sunlight streaming through large windows on a variety of toys and books that were scattered in playful disarray, the domain of the kind-hearted Nanny who had worked for the family for several years.

"Mama! Aunt Lizzie! Come see my party!" called Maggie, shaking her blond ringlets in excitement as she hugged them both happily. Then, before Lizzie could reply, the little girl grabbed her hand and led her over to a collection of porcelain dolls that were arranged in a circle on the floor around a small tea set.

The next few minutes were a whirlwind of activity, as Maggie bounced around the nursery, anxious to show Lizzie all her treasures. But then baby James, who was sleeping in a cradle at the far side of the room, began to cry, and Alison picked him up and soothed him until he settled down and began to smile up at her. Alison then motioned for Lizzie to sit in a rocking chair and placed the infant in her arms.

Lizzie stroked his downy blond hair as she rocked him and showered his perfect head with kisses. He was so beautiful, with rose-bud lips and delicate eyelashes, and her heart ached as she stared at him. As she adjusted his blanket, she noticed the embroidery on its border, and traced it with her finger. "Barbara embroidered this one."

"You both hated needle-work," Alison laughed.

"Mother said no one would marry us if we weren't proper ladies," Lizzie nodded. "But when she wasn't watching we threw aside our embroidery and dreamed of marrying gallant men who would liberate us from needles and thread!"

The memory brought poignant laughter, then she continued, "Since Barbara was older, she would marry first. She would have four children, two girls and two boys. I would have three. And they would all play together…"

Lizzie continued to smooth the blanket with a pensive frown, but it was

Alison that voiced her thoughts. "Barbara never had a chance..."

Pierced by memories of her sister's illness, Lizzie nodded sadly. Six years had passed since her death, but the ache of loss never really went away.

Lizzie was pulled from her reverie as the baby stared up at her and began to coo. She offered him a finger and he grasped it with a smile that melted her heart. When she handed him back to Alison, she watched wistfully as her friend bounced him tenderly on her knee, while Maggie clung to her. And she did not need any more words to know that for Alison, this was enough.

Chapter 14

The putrid stench was nauseating, with so many bodies crammed together in the suffocating heat. A pall of despair hung in the air, the room silent apart from occasional tense whispers, and the rattle of chains. The lethargy was worsened by hunger, as the few rotting scraps tossed into their midst a few hours earlier were the last they would see for the day.

Unable to bear the pain and fear on the faces of the other slaves, Tamar kept her eyes on Micah and Joseph, careful to mask her own anxiety for her son's sake. And although she knew that Joseph was attempting to do the same, she could read his impotent rage in the tension in his shoulders and the way he clenched his jaw. Seated on the dirt floor, she observed him as he held Micah up to the barred window of the old warehouse to see the activity in the nearby slave market.

Then, with a burst of energy, Micah wiggled from his father's arms and plunked himself onto Tamar's lap. "We'll be together, won't we Mama?"

"Course we'll be together, Micah," she soothed, trying to convey a sense of hopefulness that she did not feel. "Massa promised he wouldn't divide families."

With a trusting smile, the lad jumped from his mother's lap, and lay on his stomach at her feet. Unaware of the dismal squalor around him, he was quickly absorbed in playing with the wooden horse that his father had whittled, and some strands of straw.

With Micah's attention diverted, Tamar stood beside Joseph, appalled by the cruel scene before them. And when she could bear it no longer, she pulled him away as she grasped his right hand in both of hers. Then, running her fingers over the callouses on his palm, she kissed the tips of his fingers tenderly. Despite the constraints of his chains, he pulled her protectively into his arms, and kissed her gently on the forehead. Then softly, so that Micah would not hear, he whispered, "If we're separated ..."

She tensed in his arms, resisting his words. "But Massa promised ..."

"Micah needs his Mama," Joseph persisted.

Tamar stared at him, unwilling to admit the truth. But when she looked down at Micah, her eyes filled with tears, and with a sense of deep sorrow, she nodded at Joseph.

And Micah, feeling safe and relaxed with his parents so close, looked up at them with a contented smile, then returned happily to his simple toys.

Chapter 15

꧁ ꧂

The vibrant panes of stained glass glowed against the night sky in a palette of rich colours – a beacon of serenity in the darkness. But inside the village church the atmosphere was far from peaceful.

The pews were packed with an incongruous crowd of spectators, as peasants in drab work clothes mingled with ladies in fashionable evening dresses and gentlemen in top hats. Opinions were clearly polarized, with a vocal minority shouting their reactions as loudly as possible.

Charles was frustrated by it all and wanted to escape before it ended. But when he glanced at Lizzie beside him, she was listening intently to Tom's speech. And so, Charles reluctantly turned his attention back to the front of the room, where a large banner proclaiming EMANCIPATION compelled him to face a subject that he did his best to avoid.

"Our opponents prophecy economic doom if the slaves in the colonies are set free," Tom exclaimed. "Like Marlowe's Faust, they have traded their souls for power and profit!"

A strident barrage of competing voices forced Tom to pause.

"Here! here!"

"Emancipation would destroy trade!"

"No, he's right!"

"It will ruin England!"

Lizzie turned toward Charles, and he could see the question in her eyes.

But he avoided her gaze and stared back at Tom as he resumed dramatically, "History books record the deeds of the famous. The great reformers and the great tyrants. But hidden between the lines are countless ordinary people whose choices also change the world - for good, and for ill!"

Another wave of dissent swept through the room, and when it settled, Lizzie was visibly surprised at Tom's next words. "We are honoured to have in our midst the daughter of William Wilberforce," he announced, staring at her with an expression that Charles could not read. When Tom motioned for her to join him, Charles noticed that Lizzie seemed reluctant, and that her face flushed when he handed her a paper and continued, "Miss Wilberforce will read a letter of encouragement that Methodist leader John Wesley wrote to her father years ago, when Abolition seemed impossible."

With trembling hands, Lizzie began to read, "Unless the Divine power has raised you up to be 'against the world' I see not how you can go through your glorious enterprise in opposing that execrable villainy ..." She stumbled slightly over the words and had to catch her breath before continuing, "... which is the scandal of religion, of England, and of human nature." She looked around awkwardly at the audience, and stared briefly at Charles with a pleading expression, then held up the letter once more. "Unless God has raised you up for this very thing, you will be worn out by the opposition of men and devils, but if God be for you, who can be against you?"

Charles glared at Tom as the audience responded with a mix of applause and insults. *What hold did the man have on Lizzie,* he wondered with a stab of jealousy, *that he could exploit her so blatantly?* When Lizzie slipped quietly into the seat next to him, her tension was palpable, and she would not meet his gaze.

"Twenty years have passed since Abolition," Tom declared emphatically. "Most of us will live our entire lives in England and never see a slave. Yet our polite drawing rooms are haunted by their presence! Their blood stains our gold. Freedom is long overdue for those still enslaved under the British flag!"

The audience was in an uproar, and Charles could barely restrain himself from challenging Tom. But with Lizzie present he was depending on Stuart. *Where was the man?* he fumed. *Late as usual.*

And then a familiar voice cut through all the chaos.

"Mr. Macaulay, I feel compelled to challenge your naïve marriage of politics and religion. They make a seductive and dangerous alliance!" It was Stuart, his arguments articulate, his manner dripping with disdain and arrogance. Charles glanced back at him, relieved that his offensive character was perfectly suited to this occasion. He was standing near a pew in the back, commanding the attention of everyone in the room. Sitting beside him, dressed in an expensive gown that was far too risqué for such an event, was Rebecca, the serving girl that Stuart had met at the tavern. And when Charles saw the detached expression in her beautiful eyes, and the heavy rouge on her cheeks, he knew the change had already begun.

"Dangerous?" Tom challenged.

"The Americans had the wisdom to separate church and state in their constitution!" Stuart retorted.

"That same constitution proclaims that all men are equal!"

"Men, yes!" Stuart spat contemptuously.

"You are implying that the Africans are not human?"

Stuart surveyed the audience with a cynical smile. "How many of your high-minded reformers gathered here would sit at the same table with them?"

The response from the listeners was electric, as noisy laughter drowned out the disapproval from the reformers. Tom waited in silence until the commotion settled down, then replied with confident authority, "The Reformers of Clapham sent their children to school with free African children from Sierra Leone!"

As the audience erupted once more, Charles felt an odd sense of satisfaction at the disgusted expression on Stuart's face. But when he turned back to Lizzie, her eyes were on Tom, who was staring back at her as if they were linked by a secret language that no one else understood.

* * *

Lizzie was anxious to talk to Charles, but she had not had even a moment alone since the formal part of the evening had ended. Most of the audience had converged on the church hall – many no doubt attracted by the promise of refreshments. Tom was having a heated debate nearby with several men who opposed Emancipation. In contrast Lizzie was surrounded by a group of admirers of her father, who had only kind words for her part in the evening. But they all wanted to shake her hand and ask her to pass along personal messages to the man they so respected, which, in her current conflicted state, was almost worse than angry words. Charles could barely mask his impatience and had left her side to get some punch.

"You are a credit to your name, Miss Wilberforce," beamed a stooped old man with a kind face and twinkling eyes. "You must be very proud of your father – and of Mr. Macaulay."

Lizzie blushed deeply and, far too aware of her own hypocrisy, could barely murmur a polite response.

"It was most touching to hear you read the letter to your father," interjected a sarcastic voice from behind. Stuart!

"Don't patronize me!" she snapped, as she turned to face him, incensed by his scornful manner.

"You misunderstand me. I believe that you and I have more in common than you realize," he prodded.

"I doubt it!" she exclaimed, barely noticing that her father's admirers were uncomfortable with the confrontation and began to drift away.

Feigning concern, Stuart goaded, "But will your income not depend on the plantation?"

Silenced by the truth of his challenge, Lizzie hesitated, then stammered awkwardly, "That may change ..."

"Miss Wilberforce, may I be completely honest with you?" Stuart continued with a cynical smile.

"I would have thought you were incapable of complete honesty, Mr. Knight!" Lizzie retorted.

"I am many things," he replied sarcastically, "but I never deceive myself. I accept the deep hungers and cravings that are common to us all. Even embrace them. I have no need to lie."

"Perhaps they have mastered you!"

Stuart's gaze swept over Lizzie impertinently, before he replied with a provocative sneer, "Perhaps when we next meet, we can delve further into the topic of self-deception. A fertile ground for discussion I always find, don't you?"

Clenching her fists in frustration, Lizzie fumbled for a reply, just as Charles returned and handed her a glass of punch. But Stuart had clearly lost interest in the conversation, and with a bow to Lizzie and a brief nod at Charles, he abruptly took his leave.

"He is intolerable!" Lizzie exclaimed to Charles.

"It is pointless to argue with him," he shrugged.

Still upset, Lizzie continued to watch Stuart as he approached a lovely young woman on the other side of the room. As he put his hand on her waist to lead her out the door, Lizzie realized that she was very young, and that she seemed to take no pleasure in his company. And before they left the room, Stuart glanced back at Lizzie with an expression of arrogant contempt that shocked her to the core.

"That girl with Stuart," she frowned. "Did you know about her?"

She could see by Charles' guarded expression that he did, but Tom's arrival cut short his reply. There was a moment of awkward silence, and the tension between the two men was palpable.

Finally, Charles observed dryly, "You and Lizzie have known each other a long time."

Lizzie stared at Charles, anxious about the undertone in his words, but before she could intervene, Tom quipped, "Did she tell you we were engaged? How many times was it Lizzie? Even married once or twice."

Charles frowned at Lizzie, and she could see the anger barely below the surface. With a reassuring hand on his arm she laughed, "I was only ten years old! And Barbara and I thought Tom was a better groom than our bossy brothers!"

When Charles remained silent Lizzie continued nervously, "Tom's father worked with my father for years."

"I know," Charles replied coldly.

"Tom, tell Charles about your father's experience as governor of Sierra

Leone," Lizzie urged. "An attempt to form a free society with Africans and whites working side by side ..."

Before Tom could respond, Charles flared, "Another history lesson Tom? What of your own achievements?"

"Beware, Charles!" Tom retorted. "Your mask is slipping!"

Lizzie looked back and forth between them, distressed by their animosity. But before she could say anything further, Tom cut short the discussion. "I will wait at the carriage, Lizzie."

"How could you insult Tom like that?" Lizzie chided, as she watched him walk out the door.

"I've seen how he looks at you!" Charles snapped.

"It's not like that!" Lizzie exclaimed.

"Perhaps you care for him!"

"Tom is like a brother to me!"

Charles stared at her uncertainly, and when he finally spoke, he seemed to have mastered his emotions. "Lizzie, this evening leaves both of us with much to consider. Perhaps you need some time to decide what you really want."

And before she could think of a response, he kissed her gently on the cheek, and walked out the door.

When the driver helped Lizzie into the carriage, she and Tom sat in awkward silence for several minutes, separated by an invisible barrier that Lizzie did not know how to breach. She hated the tension between them, and desperately sought words that would help to heal the rift, but they caught in her throat, and she did not voice them.

It was Tom who spoke first. For several minutes he poured out his heart, expressing his concern for her, speaking truth into her life, and challenging her as only a sincere friend could.

But Lizzie did not want to be challenged, and she was not ready for truth, and she became defensive. And so, the rift was not mended, and she retreated to her side of the carriage in sullen silence.

Chapter 16

Tamar felt faint and did not know how much longer she could stand in the glaring sun without water. And although she and Joseph had done their best to distract Micah from the nightmare of the slave auction, he could not be soothed.

"I'm thirsty Mama," he whined, slapping her arm in frustration. "And hungry." And then, in the middle of the group of slaves that had been herded into the pen, he gave in to his pent-up emotions with a noisy tantrum.

Suddenly a strong pair of hands grabbed Tamar from behind and dragged her up onto the platform. "Mama! Mama!" Micah cried, struggling in the arms of a burly slavedriver while two other men beat Joseph to the ground with their clubs.

She wanted to scream but was too numb to speak. And when she looked at the leering white faces crowded around the platform, a rising sense of panic sucked the air from her lungs.

"We want to see more of her!" called a man near the front with an obscene gesture. The other spectators laughed and called out crude comments about her body, and what they would like to do with it. The man on the platform suddenly pulled off the kerchief that hid her hair, and when it fell around her shoulders there were more catcalls and lustful remarks.

She closed her eyes as the noise and confusion swirled around her, trying without success to block out the horror of it all. But then, another voice rose above the rest. A voice that was strangely familiar and filled her with terror. And when she opened her eyes, she was shocked to see Massa Vincent's piercing blue eyes staring at her. At his command she was lifted from the platform to stand in front of him, his smile triumphant as lascivious comments of disappointment rippled through the crowd. With a sinking heart she knew that he was her new Massa.

When a slavedriver began to lead her away, she was gripped with fear. "My husband! My son!" But Massa Vincent was unmoved by her plea, and when he shook his head, the man continued to pull Tamar toward a nearby wagon.

After a few steps she heard Joseph calling to her and wrenched from her captor's grip in an attempt to see him. When the man regained control of her chains she fell to her knees in a filthy puddle of mud and manure and began to wail in despair. With escape impossible she grabbed fistfuls of mud and began to mat her hair with them. And clutching the only act of defiance left to her she dug her fingernails into her face and scratched until it bled.

Suddenly Massa Vincent loomed over her, his face contorted in anger, and pulled her to her feet. But she had nothing left to lose and dared to look him directly in the eyes as she continued to scratch her face with her free hand. He grabbed both her wrists and stared back at her, then gestured to his slavedriver.

When Joseph and Micah were led before the Massa, Tamar felt a flicker of hope. "I'd as soon sell him as keep him!" he shouted as he pushed her son toward her. "Don't put me to the test!"

Her heart swelled with relief as Micah wrapped his arms around her legs and she sank to her knees in front of him. When his small hands gently patted her cheeks, she could no longer hold back her tears, and could taste the blood and dirt as they poured down her face.

But then Massa Vincent pushed Micah away impatiently and the slavedriver pulled her to her feet. And as he began to lead her to the wagon Tamar could see Joseph, his face swollen with bruises and creased in despair as two men hauled him away.

"Joseph!" she shouted. But he just shook his head and called, "Our boy needs his Mama!"

By the time she and Micah had been loaded onto the wagon, the men had taken Joseph away. And although she feared she would never see him again, she knew that the desolate expression on his face would haunt her forever.

Chapter 17

The man was pompous and condescending, and Charles disliked him immediately.

"The turnover has been unusually high recently," he droned, "and so we will need 150 new stock as soon as possible."

Charles was accustomed to the euphemisms that were part of the vocabulary of his business, but for some reason today the discussion grated on his nerves. His attention wandered to the rain beating against his office window, and to Lizzie, and whether she had received his message …

"… and of course, I cannot be held responsible for the sickly ones that do not pull their weight, or the rebels that use any excuse to try to escape. Do you not agree?"

The scandal of religion, of England and of human nature. The words flashed through Charles' mind without warning. Unbidden. Unwelcome. Lizzie's voice from the previous evening reading that disturbing letter …

"Mr. Pinney? Do you not agree?"

Charles forced his attention back to the annoying man sitting across from him and made a noncommittal gesture for him to continue. From everything the man had told him, he suspected that he half-starved and mistreated his slaves, and the thought of offering him a loan was highly distasteful. But he was a close acquaintance of one of Charles' most powerful investors, so what choice did he have?

Charles knew that the man had recently been to St. Kitts to visit his plantation, and there were many questions he wanted to ask. But he could not bring himself to voice them, because deep down he knew he did not want to hear the answers.

And so, he placed the document on the desk between them and watched in silence as his new client signed it with a flourish, and a self-congratulatory air.

When he had left, Charles stood near the window, absent-mindedly watching as people hurried past, seeking shelter from the rain. And when the phrase echoed again, he became defensive. *The scandal of religion.* But he had always promoted conversion of his slaves to Christianity. He even paid for a preacher to teach them. With an edited version of the Bible of course, so they would not be confused by some of those verses that the so-called Reformers liked to use.

With a sense of relief, he knew what he must do. He would write to Vincent Bartley and remind him of the high standards that he, like his father, expected for treatment of his slaves. And he would book passage for Stuart on his next ship, which would sail at the beginning of May, and send the letter with him. Because despite Stuart's usefulness to the West India Association, it was time to send him home.

Chapter 18

Despite the bumpy ride and the trauma of the day Tamar had fallen into an exhausted sleep, with Micah sprawled across her lap. When the wagon pulled to a stop near a run-down group of thatched mud huts, she was jerked awake as the slave driver picked her up and handed her down to Massa Vincent.

He removed her chains with a nod toward Micah, who was writhing in the muscular arms of the slavedriver. "Behave yourself if you want to see your brat again!" Then, after slinging a leather bag over one shoulder he gripped her wrist tightly and pulled her to the door of a nearby hut.

"Rachel," he shouted, as he pushed the door open without knocking. "Clean her up!"

A pretty woman several years older than Tamar set aside her mending, her face impassive, and led her to a stool on the far side of the tiny room.

"When she's ready, bring her to the house," Massa Vincent ordered, tossing a frilly red dress to Rachel.

When he left, Tamar had reached her limit, and sank listlessly to the dirt floor. Rachel filled a basin with water and kneeled before her, her face kind, with the hint of tears in her eyes. And with a scrap of cloth, she gently washed Tamar's face.

It took over an hour to wash her hair and bathe her. The dress was the most beautiful garment that Tamar had ever seen, but after Rachel helped her put it on, she felt uncomfortable. It was so tight in the waist that she could barely breathe. And so low-cut at the front that she felt exposed.

When she was ready, Rachel held up a broken mirror, and Tamar was amazed at the result. The scratches on her face were barely visible, and her hair was silky, and piled on her head in a style she had only seen white women wear, from a distance. And she could hardly recognize herself in the dress.

A small thrill of pleasure coursed through her but was quickly extinguished when she noticed the sadness on Rachel's face. "Beauty's a curse for the likes of us," she whispered. Tamar stared back at her, uncertain of her meaning. And then, with a sickening sense of apprehension, she understood.

When Rachel led her up to the Big House, Massa Vincent was smoking a cigar on the verandah, with a book open on his lap and a glass of rum in his hand. "Take her upstairs Rachel," he instructed. "I will join her shortly."

Tamar had never been inside the house of a white person before and was amazed that the room was so big and beautiful. When Rachel turned to leave, Tamar grabbed her hand. But Rachel could not stay, and Tamar was left alone. And as she stared at the huge bed, with 4 corner posts and a canopy of glistening material that she had never seen before, she felt sick with fear as she tried to imagine what would happen next.

Suddenly Massa Vincent threw open the door and burst into the room. And when he pulled her into his arms and carried her to the bed, she quickly discovered that the reality was far worse than she had imagined. His nails, unlike Joseph's, were clean and neat. His hands were soft. But Tamar knew from the first time he touched her that they would not be gentle.

Chapter 19

"Aunt Lizzie are you feeling better? The rain has stopped and there's a rainbow!"

Lizzie smiled at the eager voice of her nephew William and sat up in bed. The pounding headache that had confined her to her room for the day had finally passed. Wrapping a shawl around her shoulders she opened the door and stepped aside as he twirled past her like a 6-year-old tornado and climbed onto the window seat.

"Look Aunt Lizzie!" he exclaimed, pointing at the rear garden. "There are lots and lots of puddles to jump in!"

Although she wondered if her father had put him up to the offer, she could seldom refuse his childish enthusiasm and his boundless energy. And so, after donning an old smock and a pair of gardening boots, Lizzie soon found herself splashing in puddles and admiring a beautiful rainbow with the one person in her family who did not seem to be disturbed by the current crisis.

It all seems so calm, so normal, Lizzie mused as she pushed William on a swing that had been suspended from the branch of an old oak tree. Had they come to terms with her desire to marry Charles? Or was this just a temporary truce to prepare for the real battle ahead?

They had a lovely time together and then, just as her stomach began to remind her that she had not eaten all day, Mrs. Knowles appeared with a tray of tea and sandwiches and small cakes, chiding her cheerfully that, "Miss

Lizzie you've got to keep your strength up!"

"Where is everyone?" Lizzie asked.

"Master Tom left after breakfast. And your father's back was acting up, so your mother insisted they go to The Pump Room to take the waters, and your uncle went with them."

Tom has left already! Lizzie thought, disappointed that she had not been able to resolve their dispute. She would write to him, but would things ever be the same between them?

When her brother William came to reclaim a very dirty but happy boy for bed, Lizzie sat in a wicker armchair and relished the peaceful solitude as the western sky became tinged with vivid hues of pink and orange and red before the sun disappeared over the horizon in a ball of fire.

On her way back to her room she noticed an envelope on a small table in the foyer. It was in Charles' handwriting, addressed to her. *How long has it been here?* She frowned. Anxious to read it, she walked quickly up the stairs. Near the top she could hear the voice of Uncle James coming from the open door of the library. And when she heard her name, and her father's muffled reply, she sank down onto the top step and eavesdropped unashamedly.

"My thoughts are far too unsettled to read," her father remarked.

"I'm not surprised," replied her uncle.

"It is the cruelest of ironies …"

"She may yet change her mind."

She could hear the click of her father's shoes on the hardwood as he paced around the small room. "In ancient Greece, Eros was merely one of four loves. But the fierceness of his flame often eclipses the other three!"

"Aye, but Eros is known to be fickle!"

"He likes to toy with his victims …"

"What greater sport than to draw together dissimilar lovers with a beguiling passion …" Uncle James agreed.

"And when Eros tires of the game, he may leave them bound together in mutual loathing!"

Mortified by their conversation, Lizzie clenched her fists in frustration and fled down the hall to nurse her wounded pride. But before she reached her room, her father stepped into the hallway and invited, "Lizzie, would you please join us? We have something important to discuss."

With a flutter of apprehension, she entered the library and sat stiffly across from her father and Uncle James. After an awkward pause, her father began, "Lizzie, this situation has been difficult for all of us, and after talking it over with James and your mother, we came to the realization that we need to seek a voice of wisdom from outside the family."

"Wisdom?" Lizzie asked in confusion. "Whom do you propose?"

Her father exchanged a glance with Uncle James then continued "Thomas Babington. He has been such a good friend and colleague for so many years."

Thomas Babington! Tom's uncle?

"But he lives in Leicestershire. Do you plan to invite him here?"

"No, we will visit him at Rothley Temple for a few days. We will leave tomorrow after breakfast."

"Rothley Temple?" Lizzie retorted. "A few days? I cannot ..."

Cutting short her protests, Uncle James chided, "Lizzie, I am not able to join you, so I'll speak my mind now."

Lizzie sat quietly, bracing herself for her uncle's fiery temper. But he spoke gently, with obvious affection.

"Lizzie, I am ashamed of the things I did, and the people I hurt when I was young, because I seemed unable to control my passions. I hope that you will learn from my mistakes."

Flushing with embarrassment, Lizzie knew he was referring to a tumultuous time in his life when he had fallen in love with two women at once, leaving one with an illegitimate child.

"When I finally got my life into a semblance of order, I went to St. Kitt's. As you will recall, as soon as I arrived, I witnessed a horrible event. A trial of four slaves accused of murdering a white man."

Lizzie had heard accounts of her uncle's years as a lawyer on St. Kitt's many times before and they had always stirred renewed fervour for the Cause. But now things were different, and she wished she could close her ears.

"It was a nightmare that changed my life forever," he recalled, his brogue getting stronger with the rawness of his emotions. "The trial was a travesty.

And despite the lack of evidence, they were convicted – and burned alive!"

"Uncle James, I know that some plantation owners are cruel, but Charles assures me that his slaves are well cared for."

"Ach, Lass, don't be so easily fooled! Plantations with absentee owners are the worst of all!"

"I think Charles is starting to realize some things ... In time he might make changes ..."

"He has a lot to lose!"

"Would my sacrifice make any difference? I will never be a great reformer like Father."

"Your choice will make a difference to you. What you live for. What you teach your children. How you serve God."

"It always comes back to duty ... and guilt!"

Gazing at her with compassion her uncle replied, "I've met many stunted souls who make truth and goodness look dull because their motive is duty, not love. They're cloaked in self-righteousness, but it scarcely hides their bitterness!" Then, touching her arm fondly he added, "I'd hate to see you join their ranks."

Stung by her uncle's words, Lizzie was briefly speechless, then countered, "But do we really need to go to Rothley? Cannot we resolve things on our own?"

With a barely perceptible nod toward her father, Uncle James said quietly, "Your father always finds Thomas' presence so ... calming ..."

As she looked at her father the strain was clearly visible in his furrowed brow and in his stooped shoulders. And in the end her love for him won out over her anger.

When she returned to her room, she tore open Charles' letter and her pulse quickened at the tenderness of his words as he expressed his regret at the tension between them when they had parted the previous evening, and his longing to meet with her at soon as possible.

And as she took out some paper to pen a reply, she struggled to find words to explain that, despite her fervent desire to be with him, it would be several days before they could be together again.

Chapter 20

"Come have some stew," Rachel encouraged kindly, as Tamar sank down onto a small stool in the square outside the hut.

But Tamar just shook her head. She had barely managed to walk back from the Big House, and she felt too sick to eat.

She stared ahead in a trance-like state, trying to block the images from her mind, but she knew it was no use. They were too ugly. Too cruel. Too shameful. They were part of her now and she could never escape them.

When she heard Micah's cheerful voice from across the square she looked up and did her best to force a smile onto her face. He threw himself into her arms and she clung to him like she would never again let him go. And when the tears began to roll down her cheeks, she made no effort to restrain them.

It was Micah who pulled away first. "These is my new friends Mama," he told her excitedly, as he yanked on her hand. And then she noticed them. Three light-skinned children, the oldest a tall gangly youth who observed her cautiously, his expression serious and guarded. The youngest a spunky girl a couple of years older than Micah, with a golden gleam of mischief in her honey-brown eyes. And a boy in the middle with an air of curiosity and a ready smile.

"These my children," Rachel beamed proudly. "Daniel – he my oldest, Amos, and Ruthie. They's been lookin' after your boy while you …" She caught herself and averted her eyes, and at first Tamar thought she was embarrassed by what Tamar had done. Who she had become.

But then, with a shock of understanding, she looked into the eyes of the two older children who were staring up at her, and she knew that she had seen those eyes before. An intense shade of blue that matched those of Massa Vincent! And with a certainty beyond words, she sensed the bond that linked her with Rachel, and finally understood the tears glistening in her eyes.

Chapter 21

Rothley Temple had not really changed very much from previous visits, and yet nothing was the same. The long lane leading to the mansion was still lined by stately oaks. The cottages of the tenants were well cared for and reflected the fairness and generosity of Thomas Babington and his wife Jean as landowners. And, of course, the Wilberforce family received a warm welcome from their hosts.

But as Lizzie thought back to the excitement of childhood visits, she found it far too quiet, with only her parents and Robert and their two elderly servants as guests. She missed the noise and friendly rivalry of her brothers playing cricket on the green with their cousins and friends. The adventure of mock battles with wooden swords as the girls joined in to fight for control of the footbridge across the stream in the glen. And the hilarity that resulted from her brother William's water-logged attempt to float his small boat across the pond.

Every corner of the house was also haunted with bitter-sweet memories. Games of hide and seek with Tom Macaulay and his sisters. Plays that she and Barbara had created with Marianne Thornton and the other girls. Treasures they had found in the attic when rainy days kept them inside.

And Barbara – Lizzie missed her most of all. As she unpacked her clothes in the lilac-hued guest room that they had shared, her heart ached as she recalled the stifled laughter and whispered secrets that had kept them awake late into the night.

When she descended the stairs, Lizzie could hear her father's voice telling a story. Witty. Animated. Like his younger self. Thomas Babington's friendship always seemed to energize him. She was transported to a visit to Rothley over twenty years earlier, when the very air seemed charged with energy as her father met with his Abolitionist colleagues to draft the final bill for Abolition of the slave trade. Although Lizzie had not understood the details, the conversations had been intense and dramatic, and she had been gripped by an irresistible sense of excitement.

The men who had gathered around the long dining room table were her father's closest and most trusted friends, and yet they were all so different. Zachary Macaulay – Tom's father – brilliant, yet serious. So demanding and distant with Tom. Her father's cousin, Henry Thornton, was generous and diplomatic, while Uncle James' fiery temper and impatience added drama to the discussions. And Thomas Clarkson and Thomas Babington and the others had diverse personalities and divergent opinions that sometimes threatened to tear them apart. Yet her father was able to pull them all together and smooth over the conflicts with his wit and warmth – and his love for them all.

"I noticed in today's paper that Ronald Black has retired," Thomas Babington was saying as Lizzie entered the drawing room. Holding up the article he read, "Mr. Black has had a long and distinguished career as a Member of Parliament and will be missed by his colleagues and constituents."

"As I recall his main distinction was as a weathervane, flip-flopping with every political wind!" her father laughed. And then, with the talent for mimicry that had so long astounded even his foes, he began to imitate their wavering colleague. "Of course, Wilberforce, you can count on me for support. The Slave Trade is a blight on English society."

Turning his head to the right, like the motion of a weathervane, he continued, "Sorry about missing the vote for Abolition, Wilberforce, but there was a comic opera in town."

Just as quickly, he turned to the left and resumed, "Don't worry, Wilberforce. This bloody revolution in France is just a temporary set-back. We'll certainly support you next year."

Lizzie smiled as her father turned again to the right. "It can't be helped. With the war with Napoleon, I simply cannot vote for Abolition now."

Then, with a final turn to the left, her father completed the parody with a flourish. "Wilberforce, let me be among the first to congratulate you on the success of the vote. All it took was a united front."

Lizzie joined the others in appreciative laughter and felt a sense of relief to see her father in such fine form. But then she caught Robert's eyes on her – his quizzical smile a reminder of the real reason for their visit – and of her own disloyalty and vacillation.

Chapter 22

Charles stared up at the prisms of multicoloured light that streamed from the ornate window above the pulpit. The tranquil image of Christ gazing down at him with His hand raised in blessing usually gave him a sense of calm serenity. But today Charles' mind was in turmoil, and he found no comfort there.

He turned his attention to the Vicar's bland words of reassurance, hoping they would chase away his niggling doubts. The priest was certainly the right man for the job, Charles mused. Still young enough to be teachable, and well aware of the web of social and political connections that had led him to such a prestigious and highly-paid position in this wealthy and influential Church of England congregation. Astute and pragmatic enough to understand that the prosperity of Bristol depended on its thriving merchants and traders. That his role was to affirm and encourage, not to challenge or rebuke.

But today even the priest's melodious voice could not push Lizzie's letter from Charles' mind. *Wilberforce has played me false,* he fumed. *Will he go back on his word?*

Charles was furious that Lizzie's family had taken her away for the week. Apprehensive that they would force her to end the engagement. *She's been indoctrinated all her life with Wilberforce's fanatical brand of Christianity. Can she possibly stand up to her family?*

Suddenly, like a slap on the face, Lizzie's voice burst into his thoughts.

"That execrable villainy, which is the scandal of religion, of England and of human nature." For a moment the words jolted him, and he felt an uneasy sense of guilt. Was there some truth in what she had read at the Emancipation meeting?

He sat in silence, trying to reorder his thoughts. Refusing to allow such foolish questions to shake the foundation of everything he had built, he pushed away her words and forced his mind back to the soothing words of the Vicar. Safe. Comfortable. Affirming.

He looked around at the other worshipers, their clothing elegant but not ostentatious. Secure in their privilege, with no need to flaunt it. Philanthropic with their wealth without going to extremes. Protecting the future of their city by standing up to quixotic reformers and naïve idealists who had no understanding of the way things were. Of the way things had to be.

His eyes drifted once more to the face of Christ, seeking His benediction. But the sun had disappeared behind a cloud and there was a somber gravity in His expression that had not been there before. An enigmatic quality that Charles had never noticed. So that rather than basking in His blessing, Charles found that he could not meet His gaze and was forced to look away.

Chapter 23

"As you know Lizzie, your father blames himself for his misjudgments in this matter. He wants to be clear that you are free to make your own decision."

Thomas Babington's voice was gentle, his expression kind, as he waited for her response. Lizzie met his eyes awkwardly, conscious of the ticking of the gilded clock on the mantel of the library fireplace. She had known this man her entire life, and there was a reason that her father often turned to him for advice.

"You know how close I am to Father. How much I admire him and have always wanted to be true to his legacy. But now I feel like such a hypocrite!"

"Perhaps for the first time you are facing a real choice. A personal cost …"

"I know what I should do," Lizzie nodded, "but I feel so indecisive. So conflicted. So weak. I change my mind a hundred times a day!"

"I have known your father since our days at Cambridge," Thomas replied, "My respect for his brilliance, his eloquence and his devotion - not only to worthy causes, but to family and friends, and to his faith - has only grown with time."

"I thought I had inherited his passion for justice, his zeal, but I am nothing like him," Lizzie responded sadly.

"But Lizzie," Thomas smiled, "I know him well enough to know his imperfections – which he is the first to admit. His self-doubt and indecisiveness. His tendency toward vacillation and inconsistency when trying to choose a

88

course of action – not only in the political arena, but in matters of the heart!"

"Matters of the heart?" she frowned. "My parents were married six weeks after they met!"

"Yes, your mother was the first woman who won his heart, but not the first to turn his head!"

Lizzie hesitated as she considered her parents' relationship. She was much closer to her father, and often found her mother's overprotectiveness infuriating. She seemed to have no aptitude for managing a household, or for curbing her father's extravagant generosity. But there was no doubt of their deep love for one another, and of how much he depended on her for encouragement and affirmation. "You know that Mother and I are very … different …" Lizzie replied hesitantly.

"And Charles?" Thomas probed. "What is it that draws you to him?"

Lizzie could feel the blood rushing to her face as Thomas' question stirred images and emotions that she would prefer to keep hidden. Charles' hand on her waist as they waltzed together. Her passionate response when his lips met hers. The arousal in her body that kept her awake late into the night …

When she looked back at Thomas, she feared that he could read her thoughts. "My head knows what I should do," she admitted awkwardly, "but my heart …"

She looked down at her hands, at a loss for words. She could never discuss such intimate feelings with a man – even a wise and kind man like Thomas Babington. Her closest friend, Alison, had been too embarrassed to answer her questions. And Lizzie would never consider sharing her concerns with her mother.

So, she was left on her own to try to decipher the perplexing signals that left her in such a state of confusion. And although her family seemed to assume that being away from Charles might lessen her attachment to him, she discovered that with each passing day her longing for him consumed her more and more.

Chapter 24

"Papa! Papa! Where are you?"

Micah's panicked screams pulled Tamar from a restless sleep. A sleep filled with sinister ghouls with grasping claws and razer-sharp fangs …

"Hush Micah," she soothed, kneeling on the edge of his sleeping mat, and pulling him into her arms. "Mama's here."

But he stiffened against her and wrenched himself from her embrace. "Papa's hurt!" he shouted, his voice getting louder. "Papa needs help!"

Desperate to calm him, Tamar whispered urgently, "Shush Micah. You'll wake Massa Vincent."

Grasping his hand firmly, she led him out of their small hut, which was set apart from those of the other house slaves – with easy access to the Big House. "Look Micah," she pointed. "The moon is so bright. Do you think Papa is lookin' at it now just like us?"

Micah was silent as he stared intently at the big round ball in the sky. "You really think so Mama?" he asked hopefully. "You think he lookin' at the moon right now too?"

"I think so Micah. He just might be lookin' at that big yellow moon just like us. And I know he be thinkin' bout you every day, and every night."

Micah put his small hand in Tamar's and let her lead him to a rough wooden stool near their cooking fire. A few embers still glowed red, and when she stirred them, some sparks ignited, bringing the dying fire back to life. Micah snuggled against her, and after a few minutes Tamar thought he had fallen asleep. But then a soft sleepy voice broke the silence. "Mama, I miss Papa. I miss him all the time."

"I miss him too Micah. I miss him too."

"Do you think we'll see Papa soon?"

"I hope so. I sure do hope so."

His body relaxed on her lap, his breathing peaceful and calm. Finally asleep. Tamar looked down at her son's sweet face, the resemblance to Joseph stronger every day.

She missed Joseph so much. His absence was a physical ache deep inside. Like a part of her was missing.

Careful not to wake Micah, she stirred up the fire and added a few sticks of wood, wishing its warmth could thaw the coldness of her heart. Closing her eyes, she tried to recapture the image of Joseph's laughing eyes and teasing smile as he spun her in his powerful arms. She longed to feel his gentle hands soothing the tension from her shoulders. To feel the warmth of his body next to hers.

Tamar stood carefully and carried Micah back to bed. She gently covered him with his threadbare blanket, then wrapped a shawl around her shoulders and sat beside the fire for a few more minutes.

But this time when she looked into the flames, she was flooded by images of the last time she saw Joseph, his body bruised and battered. His face in agony. The moment when they were torn apart leaving a raw, gaping wound that would never heal. When she had taken Micah away, leaving Joseph alone.

A wave of guilt washed over her. Guilt for her weakness in putting her own needs for their son before Joseph's. Guilt that she had not fought harder – that she had given in. And most of all, a deep shame at who she was now. At what she had become.

Tamar's greatest desire was to see Joseph again. To be together as a family. To be his wife. But in a sickening moment of clarity, she knew it was time to face the truth. She was soiled and damaged beyond repair, and he would never be able to look at her the same way again. It was time to let him go.

Then, without warning, a surge of jealousy pierced her as she pictured

Joseph, surrounded by beautiful young slave women vying for his attention. Competing to share his bed. She hated the thought that he would not be alone for long. That she would never again feel his skin against hers ...

She stood abruptly and gazed once more at the distant orb in the sky. She would keep Micah's hope alive. The hope that some day he would see his Papa again. But she must push aside any foolish ideas that she would ever be with Joseph. That he would want her in spite of ... everything ...

Grabbing a pail of water, she dowsed the fire and stirred it until all the embers were black and cold. She pulled her shawl closer against the chill of the night, but she knew that nothing could dispel the cold ache of despair that had crept deeper into her bones. Her last flicker of hope, like the flames of the fire, now black and cold.

Chapter 25

꧁⬥꧂

Lizzie stood near the edge of the meadow and stared up at the silvery trunk of a slender birch tree. *Where is the path?* she mused. *Sam never had trouble finding it.* And then she saw it, a few feet to the right of the tree. Overgrown but still visible.

The wood was quiet apart from a gentle breeze rustling the branches and the cheerful strains of birdsong. After walking for a few more minutes, Lizzie could hear the faint sound of running water, and soon emerged from the dense shade into a sunny clearing that was traversed by a winding brook.

She looked around to get her bearings and then she saw it, near the water. The huge, flat rock that Sam had discovered on a day when he was frustrated with William's teasing, and Robert's bossiness, and their younger brother Henry's whining.

Removing her shoes and stockings, Lizzie perched on the rock and dangled her feet in the cool water. Taking Sam's letter from her pocket, she smiled as she reread it. Sweet and tender, romantic and at times naively chivalrous, it exuded the sense of anticipation that had buoyed him up since he had announced his engagement to Emily Sargent – the lively, clever and sweet-natured young woman who had captured his heart when he was still a lad of 16.

Lizzie lay back on the rock and looked up into the branches of an ancient oak tree which was covered with flowering catkins. She was happy for Sam.

She really was. And she understood his excitement and why he could not join them. But that did not make his absence any easier.

Although he was four years younger, Sam had always been Lizzie's favourite brother. She could share anything with him knowing that his kind-hearted and sensitive nature would keep it all safe. How she needed him now. She longed to tell him every detail of what had transpired in the past few days. All the heated conversations and family drama. Her anger toward Robert and her frustration with their mother. Of her love and respect for their father, and guilt for the added strain this situation had placed on his already over-burdened shoulders.

She sat up, lifted her skirts, and made her way through the shallow water to the other side of the brook. *Where is Sam's tree?* she wondered as she walked a short distance into the woods. *It was a hazelnut ...* When she saw it, she walked around the trunk until she found what she was seeking. A large heart carved into the bark, with the initials S W and E S in the centre.

She traced the heart with her finger, wondering if she would ever be able to carve a heart of her own. How she wished she could talk with Sam about Charles. Her longings and the way she felt when they were together. Her hopes for the future. Her fears and confusion. The turmoil of her emotions, and her inability to come to a decision.

But in the end, her love for her brother won out. As she waded back across the brook, she realized that she could not allow her own confusion to tinge the excitement he was feeling about his engagement. And so, when she penned her reply, she would enter joyously into his sense of celebration, and give only a vague description of her own struggles.

Chapter 26

"Will Miss Wilberforce be joining you? We are so looking forward to meeting her."

Is everyone going to ask about Lizzie? Charles seethed, irritated by the evident curiosity of the well-dressed merchants and their guests who hovered around him. But with a forced smile he replied pleasantly, "She sends her regrets, but had a family commitment that necessitated a change in plans."

"It would have been quite a coup to have the great Liberator's daughter grace us with her presence," Gavin Meeks, the Society's treasurer, persisted smugly.

"What a tantalizing idea," smirked Reginald Campbell. "The Wilberforce name associated with The Anchor Society!"

Charles had never really liked Reginald. During Charles' tenure as President of the Society a few years previously, he had found the man pretentious and vain, using his considerable influence to challenge many of the proposals that Charles had championed. He suspected that such veiled antagonism resulted from his resentment of Charles' success not only in business, but as a Bristol Councillor.

"Our program will begin shortly. Please help yourselves to some refreshments, then take your seats." The announcement by Graham Watts, the outgoing President, cut short the conversation as the guests gravitated toward the appetizing assortment of pastries on the refreshment table.

As Charles took his seat he looked around, reminded of the Emancipation meeting a few days ago. Lizzie had been nervous. Distracted. Clearly preoccupied with Tom Macaulay. The tension in the room had been palpable. The mixture of cultured society with outspoken labourers incongruous. Macaulay's claims naïve and unrealistic. Yet Lizzie had seemed to be under his spell.

A portly man smelling strongly of snuff and a pungent, and very unpleasant, cologne, sat beside Charles in the seat where Lizzie should have been. An aching sense of disappointment – and loneliness – washed over him. He had looked forward to having Lizzie join him at the meeting. To have her beside him. And to give her the opportunity to see for herself some of the worthy causes he supported.

"I will do my best to continue to honour the example of Edward Colston, whose generous philanthropy is seen throughout Bristol." Charles forced his attention back to the speaker, realizing that the new President for the year had already been introduced. "His support for almshouses, schools for the poor, hospitals and Church of England parishes in Bristol made an enormous impact during his life. Those familiar with our history will recall that at the inaugural meeting of our Society in 1769, 46 years after Edward Colston's death, 22 men dined at the Three Tuns tavern, and were so inspired by his example that they took up a collection to be donated to charity. During the early years those donations saved countless lying-in women and poor orphaned females from a life of vice and degradation."

Charles mind wandered as the speaker droned on with a tediously detailed account of the Society's history. As he glanced around at the audience, he met the gaze of an elegant silver-haired woman sitting on the far side of the room. Sarah Millard. An unpleasant image flashed through his thoughts of his mother, her eyes filled with tears. How many times had her attempts to be accepted in Bristol society been spoiled by the gossip and coldness of Mrs. Millard and her elite social circle? Although no one would ever say it to her face, how many people had believed the lies they spread about the purity of his mother's blood line? The insinuation that since she had been born in the West Indies, somehow slave blood must have tainted her lineage.

A wave of polite applause rippled through the room, drawing Charles back to the present. "Over the years we have supported a variety of excellent causes," the President concluded. "This year we have decided to contribute to the Colston's School for boys. And we hope that you will support this project generously with your donations."

Charles felt a surge of pride at the enthusiastic response to the opportunity to contribute to this admirable cause. He wished Lizzie were here to be part of this moment. To see for herself the good that was being done by Bristol's prosperous merchants.

But then he was gripped with a sense of uncertainty. The source of Edward Colston's enormous wealth was never discussed at The Anchor Society meetings. It would be unseemly to mix their philanthropy with work of the West India Association, although the income of everyone in the room most likely depended on the success of the Association in opposing Emancipation.

Am I fooling myself? Charles wondered. *Would Lizzie ever feel comfortable around these people? Would they ever accept her?*

Pushing aside his pensive mood, he joined a cluster of influential men who were helping themselves to more refreshments. And although he did not fully trust any of them, or consider them real friends, his wealth and political connections would ensure that his mother's experience would not be repeated in his own life.

Chapter 27

"You wrote to her? Without asking me first?" Lizzie exclaimed, bringing her mare to an abrupt halt in the shadow of a huge walnut tree on the edge of a tranquil meadow. "Mother, how could you?"

An awkward expression of embarrassment flitted across her mother's face as she reined in her own mount. But then, without acknowledging any fault, or pausing to take a breath, she launched into a detailed narrative. "Mary Ames seems like such a kind and devout woman. Her work with schools for poor children here in England reflects a charitable spirit. I assured her that your Father and I understand that she and her brother did not initially choose the role in which they now find themselves in relation to the West Indies, and that no doubt they would be amongst the first to rejoice if no such system existed."

Lizzie was at a loss for words, trying to imagine what Mary Ames would say to Charles about the letter. And how he would react. Tense with frustration, Lizzie demanded, "What else did you say?"

"I attempted to convey the reasons for our initial misjudgment of the situation. That we had been informed that Mr. Pinney was not a Proprietor who owned lands and slaves but only a West India Merchant. But that we have since learned that a West India Merchant is placed in the unhappy situation that his mortgages lead to the labour of the slaves on the estates to which he lends money. And that even a humane merchant had little influence to provide for the benefit and comfort of the slaves, so that mortgages uphold the system of slavery, and in many respects all the worst parts of the system in the West Indies."

"You put all that into a letter?" Lizzie fumed. "How could you write so directly without discussing it with me first?"

"I have formed a good rapport with Mary Ames and felt sure she would be receptive to my explanation, particularly after our preliminary correspondence to facilitate the meeting between you and Charles."

Lizzie stared at her mother in dismay. "What are you saying? Charles and I first met at the Twelfth Night Gala. Did you arrange that?"

"No, it was afterwards. Your father and I met Mary Ames and her sister at several social gatherings in Bath and they said they had met you ..."

Lizzie shook her head, appalled by the revelation. "So, the invitation to help at the charity event for the school ..."

Oblivious to her daughter's distress, her mother continued, "Yes, and then you joined Charles and his sisters on the outing to see their school ..."

Lizzie frowned as she tried to comprehend her mother's role in her relationship with Charles. "And Father? Did he know about all this?"

"He was so concerned for you. Your sadness since Barbara died. Your loneliness. When I told him you might not be alone much longer he was so happy. And he was busy and anxious with work and his health and the move to Highwood and William's debts ... Perhaps we did not ask as many questions as we should have."

Bewildered and uncertain, Lizzie was overwhelmed by a wave of queasiness and a dull ache in her temples.

"Lizzie, I was really trying to ..."

"Enough Mother! No more explanations!" And without another word Lizzie turned away and gave her horse free rein all the way back to the stable.

She could imagine her mother, mounted on the Babingtons' fine horse, looking after her – disappointed that the ride that she had hoped would bring them closer together had ended so badly. But Lizzie was not surprised that, despite her mother's good intentions, they just did not seem able to speak the same language.

Chapter 28

"No, the spoon go here and the little fork on the other side," giggled Ruthie, her small fingers nimble as she rearranged the silverware. "And this big fork beside it."

Tamar shook her head in frustration, then smiled back at the child's playful grin. "Easy for you!"

"You'se just not used to the way white folks eats Mizz Tamar."

"Everything so different," she agreed, awed by the elegant dining room that was larger than the hut where she and Joseph and Micah had lived. The cupboard filled with more pretty cups and bowls and plates than she had ever seen in her life. And the wood floor so smooth and shiny – nothing like the rough packed dirt of slave shacks.

"Hurry up and finish your lesson," Rachel smiled, entering from the kitchen house behind the main house with a pile of freshly ironed tablecloths and napkins. "Dinah be needin' Ruthie soon to go fetch some tomatoes for supper."

Tamar smiled back at Rachel, grateful for her help in so many ways. Learning to be a house slave was much more difficult than she had expected, even though Massa Vincent insisted that she avoid any heavy kitchen work that would callous her hands. And he still expected her to be available whenever he wanted her.

Tamar straightened her starchy black uniform and waited as Ruthie scattered the forks and knives and plates and spoons on the table. She stared at them, then closed her eyes, trying to get a picture of the way Ruthie arranged them. And this time when she finished Ruthie clapped her hands happily. "You did it Mizz Tamar! You did it!'"

Tamar flushed with pleasure as the little girl added, "You'se ready to learn 'bought polishin' the silver tomorrow!"

The sound of hurried footsteps in the front hallway ended the peaceful moment. "He's ridin' up the drive, Mizz Tamar," warned Rachel's son Amos, who had been posted as a lookout. "Massa Vincent almost here!"

Tamar turned abruptly, hoping to escape into the kitchen, but it took Massa Vincent only a few moments to throw the reins of his horse to Daniel, who was waiting for him on the front verandah. "Tamar, I will need you this evening," he instructed as he came up behind her.

She turned toward him reluctantly, eyes lowered, her face barely masking her revulsion.

"I have invited a few friends for drinks," he smiled, grasping her chin, and forcing her to look at him. "Go get cleaned up. Change out of that hideous uniform. And put on the green silk – it brings out your eyes."

"And Rachel," he ordered, "send for Tobias to draw my bath, and to set out my clothes for this evening."

It was only after he left the room, taking the stairs of the long staircase two at a time, that Tamar realized that she had been holding her breath and that her back was stiff, her muscles tense. And that despite the benefits of being a house slave, she would willingly return to the backbreaking work in the fields in her rough homespun rags if she could escape Massa Vincent's hold on her.

* * *

"I thought you were courting Amanda Gibbons, Vincent," smirked the plump man called Cox, gesturing at Tamar. "Does Miss Gibbons know about your latest acquisition?"

"Don't be a fool," sneered Vincent. "You know as well as I do that half the men on the island keep doxies. Sensible wives soon learn to accommodate to the needs of their husbands."

Cox, and a big burly man named Briggs, responded with ribald laughter, which grated on Tamar' nerves. Vincent and his three visitors had spent the past hour drinking rum and talking plantation business that she did not understand. But when they tired of more serious topics, Cox and Briggs made crude remarks about Tamar, and how the green folds of silk revealed the curves of her body. And of what they would like to do with her if she belonged to them.

But she noticed that the third guest, Styles, a small red-faced man who was losing his hair, seemed uncomfortable with their crude humour. She observed him curiously, wondering if he would challenge them. But he never did. When the others made degrading comments about her, he would simply look down at his hands, and never broke his silence. And although Tamar could feel hatred for the other brutes coiled in the pit of her stomach, she almost felt sorry for this weak, sad little man.

"Come fill my glass girl," Briggs ordered rudely. She approached him reluctantly, and before she could comply, he grabbed her free hand and ran his fingers across it. "She has the hands of a field slave," he leered. Then, moving his hand up her arm toward her neck he added, "but her body ..."

Tamar stiffened involuntarily, her eyes burning with rage. Then, as she wrenched her arm from his grasp, she could not resist tipping the bottle and splashing rum onto his white suit.

Briggs jumped to his feet, his hand raised in fury, ready to enforce his authority. She held her breath, waiting for the blow, but before he could slap her, Vincent laughed, "I told you I won't share this one."

Briggs stared back at Vincent then sat down with a stiff smile. "Watch your finances Vincent, or you may lose your prize!"

Vincent smiled smugly, then stood and put his arm around Tamar's waist, pulling her toward him. "You can wait for me upstairs in the boudoir. And change into the scarlet chiffon peignoir. With the perfume that just arrived from France."

Tamar flushed with shame at the way Massa Vincent had flaunted her in front of his friends. She was disgusted by the unconcealed lust on Briggs' face, and the profane words that emerged from Cox's mouth. The awkward passivity of Styles, who sat in strained silence and never said a word. But as she turned to flee from them all into the house, Massa Vincent's words echoed in her mind. She hated the thought of being his doxy but could not escape the truth that this ugly word conveyed what she had become.

Chapter 29

There are many things I want to teach you.

In the clear light of day Lizzie knew what she should do. Her mind ruled her emotions and she felt stronger. More determined. Able to face her own frailty and even conquer it.

But after dark, as she lay alone in the big bed that she had once shared with her sister, she was awash with images and sensations that made a mockery of her earnest resolve. His hand on her waist. The intensity in his eyes. His lips on hers …

There are many things I want to teach you.

She could barely breathe, her body burning with desire … Desire … but for what? What did it all mean? What were the secrets that Charles was so anxious to teach her and that her body was so desperate to learn?

She sat up in bed and tried to get control of her unruly passions. To stuff them back down where they belonged. To master them with the strength of her will. She threw back the coverlet and walked over to the window seat, pushing back the curtains to reveal the moonlit garden below. How many times had she sat here with her sister, whispering secrets, and telling tales that they would confide to no one else? Laughing at their mother's foibles. Plotting how to turn the tables on their irritating brothers. Shaking their heads affectionately at their father's soft-heartedness and unrestrained generosity. At the chaos of their unusual household as he kept on infirm servants well past their prime and welcomed an odd assortment of mismatched visitors – rich and poor – around their table.

The garden was still apart from the eerie call of a lonely owl and the rustle of the wind in the trees. Lizzie smiled as she thought of summer evenings chasing fireflies. Of afternoon tea with tiny china cups and cucumber sandwiches on the manicured lawn. Hide-and-seek with a troupe of noisy children after dark. The gentle fall of snowflakes that transformed the drab browns and grays of winter into a magical wonderland. And Barbara, healthy and vibrant in the midst of it all, with her whole life and all her dreams still ahead of her.

Lizzie wondered what Barbara would say about Charles. About her conflict between head and heart. About what it all meant.

But then, unbidden, another image appeared. Barbara, weak and pale, barely able to sit up in bed. Seldom complaining at the end, reassuring her anxious parents of her steadfast Christian faith. The vain attempts of the doctors to save her from the consumption that ravished her body. The White Death that snatched her away with such cruelty from the family that loved her.

How can I be so selfish? Lizzie frowned. *Allowing my emotions to distract me when Barbara never ...*

She shook her head and stood up with renewed resolve. She knew what she should do. She did not need to dwell on her frailties. It was time to make a decision and to do what was right.

She crawled back into bed and tried to sleep. But her mind was still conflicted, and when she closed her eyes, she saw his face and felt his touch. And against her will, her body responded to his whispered words.

There are many things I want to teach you.

When she finally slept, she dreamed of her wedding night, her body alive with anticipation as Charles picked her up in his arms and took her to his bed for the first time.

Chapter 30

As a rule, Stuart did not respond well to ultimatums – or to authority of any kind for that matter. Over the years he had honed his innate powers of perception and persuasion and had developed an impressive repertoire of approaches to convey his distaste for such intrusive conduct. Yet although he was an inveterate gambler – literally and metaphorically – he was also a survivor, and he knew when to fold his cards.

And so it was not by accident that he found himself on a cloudy Wednesday in late April at the offices of his employer, Mr. Charles Pinney, at the inconvenient hour of 20 minutes past 9:00 in the morning – not only on time, but a full ten minutes early. Moreover, he was impeccably attired and had donned an earnest aura of businesslike decorum that would no doubt smooth over any strain that might have crept into their relationship. And thanks to Gerald's timely warning, he was prepared to overlook the foul mood of said employer and – as much as it pained him – to resist all references to the hapless dalliance with Miss Elizabeth Wilberforce.

When a clerk showed Stuart into Charles' office it was 25 minutes past the designated time of meeting, but Stuart exuded an air of calm patience. He sat quietly on the upholstered chair across from his employer and held his tongue while he waited for Charles to look up from the papers he was reading. Of course, given his prodigious powers of observation, the delay gave Stuart time to scan the room to make a mental note of any detail – no matter how small – that might become useful in the future. Yet despite his careful preparation, Stuart was caught off guard by what happened next.

"Knight, it is time for you to return to Nevis," Charles declared decisively. "You have served your purpose and have now become a liability. I have booked your passage on one of my ships for the 5th of next month."

Stuart stared back at Charles, speechless at this unforeseen turn of events. He had expected to remain in England for several more months and did not want to return to Nevis so soon. A barrage of protests flooded his mind and he grasped for a response that would be compelling enough to change Charles' mind.

But then, with a flash of insight, Stuart realized that there was something different about Charles – a side to him that he had never seen before. Determined. Unyielding. Dispassionate. And that he was watching Stuart attentively. Waiting for his response. Expecting him to resort to his usual verbal tactics. A shift that forced Stuart to admit that there might have been a few occasions when he had pushed Charles too far.

Stuart was many things, but he was no fool, and he refused to degrade himself by bargaining, or to persist with a losing hand when the stakes were high.

And so, Stuart simply responded pleasantly, "I will be ready," scoring a small victory at the flicker of surprise on his employer's face.

"I will prepare a file of important documents for you to take to Vincent. And a letter. All confidential. With the seal to be broken only by Vincent himself."

"Confidential. Yes of course," Stuart replied gravely, relishing the fact that Charles had placed the power back in his hands. Was he really unaware that Vincent kept no secrets from him?

As he rose to leave, Stuart could not resist one tiny act of defiance. He had spied a familiar volume on a nearby bookshelf and pointed to it with an air of reverence. "I notice that you have a copy of the Slave Bible. Your father sent us a few copies several years ago and it has been enormously helpful in encouraging a docile and cooperative attitude among the slaves."

Charles frowned slightly as he reached for the book. "Father would be glad to know that it is so useful, but he always called it by its proper name: Select Parts of the Holy Bible for the use of the Negro Slaves in the British West-India Islands. Do you have sufficient copies, or shall I send more back with you?"

"More copies would certainly be put to good use. And we could pass any extras along to other plantations."

"I will have them ready when you sail." Charles promised, clearly pleased with this act of benevolence.

As Stuart took his leave, he reveled in the irony that such a powerful and successful man could have so little understanding of what really took place on the plantations that were the source of his wealth. And that ultimately Charles depended on Vincent and himself to shield him from the more unsavoury day-to-day details, so that he could enjoy the benefits and still cling to his pious illusions.

Chapter 31

"We have been here an entire week, Lizzie," Robert prodded. "Surely you have decided by now."

Lizzie tensed, ready to lash out at her brother's intrusion, but was interrupted by her father's gentle nod. "We really do need to return to Bath," he affirmed. "I was hoping to depart the day after tomorrow."

The Babington's excellent cook had made roast beef with Yorkshire pudding, Lizzie's favourite meal, but she had barely managed a few bites. She pushed aside her plate and looked at the expectant faces around the table. And as much as she hated to admit it, she knew that they were right. They had stayed at Rothley long enough and it was time to go home.

"I have reached a decision," she replied tentatively.

"Really?" her mother interrupted. "We are so anxious to hear it."

"I have decided that I need to talk to Charles before I can be sure. Not by letter but in person."

"In person?" her father probed, his brow furrowed with concern. "Do you think that is wise?"

"It has already been such a confusing and emotional time, even at a distance," Thomas agreed.

"A letter would be much easier," her mother added. "You could lay out all your thoughts and concerns in an orderly fashion ..."

"Like the letter you wrote to Charles' sister?" Lizzie snapped. "It only added to the confusion!"

When Lizzie saw the tears glistening in her mother's eyes, she regretted her harsh words. Why did she always react to her like this? There was a flicker of pain on her father's face as he put a reassuring hand on his wife's arm, a visible reminder that by hurting her mother she had hurt him as well.

"I am sorry Mother," Lizzie conceded. "I do appreciate your concern."

"We are all concerned Lizzie," her father replied. "We only want what is best for you. A husband who will not only provide for you, but with whom you can share your hopes and dreams, your joys, and trials. A partnership that will help you both to grow in your faithfulness to Christ."

"I want those things too Father," Lizzie replied, her voice barely above a whisper. "And I hope that Charles does too."

"And if he doesn't …?" Robert began, but he was silenced by their father's stern look. For several moments no one spoke, as they concentrated on the food on their plates. It was Jean Babington who broke the awkward silence. "I think Lizzie is right," she offered gently. "If she is still struggling to make such a life-altering decision, she must meet with Charles in person. And it would only be fair to Charles, whatever path she chooses."

And so, it was decided. Lizzie's father would write to arrange a meeting soon after their return – with an appropriate chaperone of course. And they would leave Rothley after an early breakfast two days hence.

Lizzie's stomach fluttered in anticipation at the thought of being with Charles again. With apprehension as she wondered how he would receive her. What she would say. How he would respond. And with uncertainty because, despite everything that had happened in their week at Rothley, she still felt just as ambivalent about her future as when they had arrived.

Chapter 32

The path was steep and treacherous, choked with thick vines and sharp brambles. The atmosphere pulsed with agonized wailing and the menacing beat of drums, as a ghostly mist swirled around stunted, misshapen trees. A bitter wind whipped the branches and tore at Lizzie's white velvet cloak as she stumbled through the murky darkness, searching in vain for a familiar landmark.

Suddenly a twisted shape that she had mistaken for a tree stood erect, brandishing a wooden sword. She jumped back in alarm, shocked at the black mask of the grim Harlequin-like figure – costumed not in colourful diamonds, but in shades of black, white and grey.

"Keep your morality to yourself!" he shouted. "Your reforms would have our nation bankrupt, and workers rioting in the streets!"

And then, with a surge of relief, Lizzie heard a familiar voice. "I feel my inadequacy for the task, but I march forward in the full assurance that my cause will bear me out ..."

"Father! Where are you?" she called.

"... the total abolition of the slave trade!" he exclaimed.

And then she saw him, as she remembered him in his prime. Standing up for truth with dignity and courage ...

A noisy cacophony of insults taunted him from all directions at once, as more masked challengers appeared and lent their wooden swords to the chaotic battle.

"You have a great affection for the fat, lazy ..."

"... and laughing and singing and dancing ..."

"... slaves ... You unfeeling ..."

"... cold-blooded ..."

"... hypocrite!"

Distressed by the anguish on her father's face, Lizzie ran toward him, but her path was blocked by the jostling crowd. When she finally managed to force her way through, she tripped on a vine and lost her shoe. Pushing herself to her feet she stumbled forward a few steps, then looked around in confusion. Where was he?

"Never, never will we desist till we extinguish every trace of this bloody traffic, which is a disgrace and dishonour to this country." When Lizzie heard her father's declaration, she tossed her other shoe aside and ran toward him with renewed determination. But suddenly he was surrounded by a swarm of hecklers who threatened him with their swords and jeered at him mercilessly.

"Slavery ..."

"... like pain in surgery ..."

"... and childbirth ..."

"... are deplorable necessities ..."

... "for which no answer ..."

"... has yet been discovered."

Lizzie was desperate to go to him, but her path was obstructed as the hostile mob encircled her father, channeling the hateful voice of William Cobbett, one of his most vicious opponents.

"Go Wilberforce ..."

"... begone, for shame ..."

".... Thou dwarf with big resounding name!"

They hemmed him in from all sides, poking him with their swords, their laughter cynical and cruel. Shocked by the intensity of the battle Lizzie ran toward her father, heartened by the relief on his face when he saw her.

But then, unexpectedly, a familiar figure appeared through the mist. Tall and confident, clothed in formal attire with a crimson waistcoat and an elegant black satin cloak. And despite the white mask on the upper part of his face, Lizzie's body came alive when she saw him, and she knew without a doubt that it was Charles.

When he extended his hand toward her, she glanced back uncertainly at her father, then, stifling a pang of remorse, she turned away and walked toward Charles. Suddenly, without warning, he reached over and ripped off her cloak, tearing the brooch that latched it at her throat from the fabric. As the pure white velvet fell onto the ground in a crumpled pile, the brooch that she had prized for so many years fell with it and was lost in the folds of discarded material. And she was left exposed. Her silky crimson dress low-cut and seductive. The sapphire necklace sparkling as garish coloured lights began to flash through the shadows. Ashamed by the mocking smiles and suggestive comments of the bawdy rabble that gawked at her every move.

But then Charles offered her a lacy white half mask on a stick, and as she held it before her face her doubts and shame faded away. With pounding heart, she grasped Charles' extended hand, following him onto a path that was broad and smooth and inviting, surrounded by friendly onlookers who affirmed her decision with nodding heads and gleeful smiles.

Suddenly Lizzie was startled by a snake which slithered across the path. She dropped her mask in horror when it reared up and hissed at her, and the spectators shrieked with terror and fled into the shadows. But before the serpent could strike, Charles grasped it firmly behind its head until it lay still in his hand. Then, unsheathing his sword, he cut open the snake, revealing a dagger with sapphires gleaming on the hilt. When Charles held the bloody snake out to her Lizzie stared at it in confusion, then cautiously removed the dagger and balanced it on her open palms. As he tossed the dead snake onto the ground, Lizzie turned uncertainly toward her father, but he had disappeared into the mist. When she looked back toward Charles, the mist began to swirl around him, until he also vanished, and she was left holding the dagger by its handle. She turned slowly in a circle, mesmerized by the jeweled blade, as the discordant mixture of drumming and wailing became steadily louder and louder, filling her with dread. Then suddenly it ended and there was only silence and an all-consuming and fearsome darkness.

For several moments Lizzie hovered at the border between sleep and wakefulness, trying to capture the threads of her dream before they unravelled completely. When she opened her eyes, her mind was unsettled as she recalled the vivid images. The crimson dress hidden beneath her white velvet cloak. The lacy white mask that changed her perspective so completely. And most disconcerting, the mangled snake, and the jeweled dagger.

With a flutter of nervous excitement, she shrugged aside the disturbing images as she recalled the significance of this day – and the importance of careful preparation. She had already laid out a lovely plum-coloured dress and a new silk shawl that went perfectly with the sapphire necklace.

As she sat before her dressing table to style her hair, Lizzie picked up a cameo of Charles – a recent and very accurate portrait that had been a constant reminder of how much she missed him during her time at Rothley. A symbol of her hopes and dreams for their future. And now the day had finally arrived. The day on which she must make the decision that would affect the rest of her life. And although she tried to push the dream from her mind, she could not help wondering what it portended for this fateful day.

Chapter 33

Charles seemed so formal. Distant. Even cold. Lizzie's hand shook slightly as she accepted a cup of tea, dismayed at the awkward silence between them.

She had anticipated this moment day and night for the past week. The warmth on his face when their eyes met. The exhilarating awareness of his nearness. Her hopes and dreams for a future together. But now ...

It was Charles who spoke first, his voice strained. His words clipped. Like he was speaking to a stranger.

"I trust you had a refreshing time away," he probed, watching her intently. "No doubt you had many edifying conversations that brought clarity to *your* dilemma."

Stung by the way he emphasized the word "your," Lizzie fumbled for a reply. "I was not ... It was ... difficult ... and lonely ..."

"Difficult? Lonely?" he snapped, the anger clear in his eyes. "And what of the way your family has behaved toward me?"

"Charles, I ..."

"And your mother's letter to my sister!" he raged. "Did she think I would not read it? The offensive intentions heightened by her pious words!"

"She sent it without my knowledge," Lizzie pleaded. "I was furious with her when I found out!"

"Then why did you not write?"

"Thomas felt that I needed time apart ... so I could ... think."

Charles considered Lizzie's words with a thoughtful frown, then his expression softened. "Perhaps we were naïve to imagine that your family would ever agree."

"They told me that I could decide for myself!"

Charles stared back in surprise, then sat near to her on the brocade settee and gently took her hand. "And so, what have you decided?"

"Nothing has changed," she breathed, her desire for him clear in her eyes.

When he began to kiss the side of her neck she protested, "Ann is in the next room!"

"Barton is keeping her occupied with tea in the kitchen," he smiled as he pulled her into his arms and kissed her softly on her lips. She could barely breathe as her body melted into his embrace, longing to experience fully what she had only dreamt about. Sure that if Charles asked her to elope with him that very day, she would not be able to refuse.

When he pulled away, she felt a pang of disappointment. "I do not want to compromise your reputation," he smiled, helping her to her feet, and leading her through the foyer out to the garden. It was a breezy day, the sky filled with dark glowering clouds. The scent of rain in the air.

As Charles linked his arm through hers and led her along a flagstone path through ornamental shrubs and well-tended flowerbeds, she smiled at the thought of herself as mistress of this fine mansion. Managing the staff. Creating a haven for Charles from the demands of his work. Raising their children. Welcoming guests …

"Charles," she asked tentatively. "Do you have many social obligations? Do you entertain a lot?"

"Yes, of course," he smiled. "And as my wife, you would have the opportunity to add your own touches."

As she considered his words, her mind was flooded by unpleasant images. The enemies of her father scowling at her at social gatherings. Their wives who would greet her with pretentious smiles, then gossip about her behind her back. And the shallowness of people like Agatha Bexhall, who would no doubt fawn and flatter only because of the wealth and power wielded by her husband.

"You seem distracted," Charles observed when she did not reply.

"I am not sure your friends would welcome me. I am from a completely different world."

"You will adjust quickly," he assured. "And they will accept you because they respect me."

"Respect?" she mused. "Respect is certainly important, but what about friendship? What do your closest friends think of me? Do they support your plans for our marriage?"

"Friends?" Charles replied hesitantly. "Like most men our conversations focus more on business and current events than on personal matters."

Startled by his words, Lizzie was reminded of the gatherings that she had attended with Charles. Overwhelmed by so many new people, she had not really thought much about the superficiality of the conversations at the time. But now she began to wonder ...

"But there must be a few ..." she commented. "Father has so many colleagues who are also his closest friends. They encourage one another. Share their joys and sorrows. Chastise one another when needed. And they are faithful no matter what they face."

"You must know by now that I am not like your father!" Charles flared. "Will you always compare me with him?"

"I am sorry. I did not intend ..."

"The real question, Lizzie, is whether your father and your family will be able to accept me!"

"Father will be true to his word. Once you get to know him you will see ..."

"But I suspect that despite good intentions he will be unable to resist his desire to reform me!"

"He is always fair – and gracious ..."

"You cannot help but defend him!" Charles countered. "But when we marry, your first loyalty will be to me. To our family. To my charities ... and my work."

"Of course, Charles, but ..."

"Lizzie can you honestly say that you will be as supportive of me as you have always been of your father and his ... causes?"

Lizzie pulled her shawl around her, conscious that the chilly day had cooled her fevered emotions. "I want so much to spend my life with you Charles," she began tentatively. "But I wonder if our differences are too great ..."

Suddenly a dramatic flash of lightening split the sky, heralding a torrential downpour. Charles grabbed Lizzie's hand as they hurriedly retraced their steps. When they re-entered the parlour, he led her over to a cheerful fire, and took her drenched shawl. After removing his own wet overcoat, he rang for Barton, who promptly arrived with a tray of tea and cakes.

Embarrassed by her disheveled state, Lizzie stared into the fire and commented, "The elements are against us."

With a tender smile Charles turned her face toward his and wrapped his arms around her. "The storm will pass."

"And what of tomorrow?"

"No one can predict the future."

"It does not take a diviner ..."

"We can be happy together."

Lizzie closed her eyes and leaned toward Charles, soaking up his warmth in contented silence. And when he gently tucked a damp curl behind her ear, she could feel her doubts fading away.

It was Charles who broke the spell. "Lizzie, I have something to show you," he invited. Grasping her hand, he led her up a flight of stairs to the library – a spacious room with views of the Frome River and the harbour beyond. With visible excitement, Charles guided her over to a long table on which were spread several drawings, as well as a detailed map of Bristol.

"They are only preliminary designs," Charles smiled. "By one of the best architectural firms in England!"

"What are they for?"

"A house. Far grander than this one. There is property in the Clifton district that might be suitable."

Lizzie stared at the plans, trying to make sense of the hand-written notations of the architect, and at the scale on the bottom of each page. "It looks much larger than this house."

"Yes, larger and more elegant – with top-quality materials and furnishings."

Frowning at the drawings, Lizzie was at a loss for words. The house Charles had inherited from his father was finer than many of the houses in which she had lived with her parents over the years. The stability of growing up in the same house a marked contrast with the frequent moves of Lizzie's family due to their financial constraints. Worst of all had been the ill-conceived purchase of Highwood Hill two years ago. A property so unsuitable that they had been forced to live for several months in rental properties in Bath. Although her mother enjoyed the social life there, as well as visits from William and his family, it was only a temporary solution to the problem.

Conscious that Charles was waiting for a response, Lizzie ventured hesitantly, "The house looks lovely Charles. But I don't understand … This house is your family home. You were born here. It must be filled with memories." Blushing self-consciously, she added. "And it has more than enough space for a family … and for children."

"There are other considerations. Other responsibilities … other expectations …"

"Expectations?"

"Influence comes at a cost. If I am to go farther in the political sphere, beyond being a Bristol Councillor, I must cultivate alliances with the elite of our society!"

"You have mentioned your political ambitions before, Charles, but perhaps I did not fully understand …"

"You of all people must be familiar with what goes on behind the scenes!"

"Of course," she probed. "But men enter politics for a variety of reasons."

"Another comparison with your father?" he flared, the offense clear in his voice.

"I am not making a comparison Charles or questioning your motives."

But with a queasy sense of anxiety, she wondered. *Do I really trust his motives? His drive for social and political prominence? His need to acquire more wealth …?*

"I expected you to be more excited about the designs Lizzie," Charles chided, disappointment clear in his voice. "Most women would be thrilled at the prospect of such a magnificent home."

"Most women?" she retorted. "I thought you knew me well enough to understand that I do not need an ostentatious mansion to be happy!" And in her irritation, the words that had hovered below the surface tumbled out unfiltered and hung in the air between them. "Especially one built on wealth obtained … in such a way."

"You have never understood," Charles retorted. "Pinney and Case is my father's legacy. When my brother John made a mess of running it, I promised Father that I would do my best to ensure that the firm that he had worked so hard to establish would flourish and thrive."

"I know how important it is to you Charles. But you are already prosperous. Do you really need more wealth? Could you not sell your plantations and invest elsewhere?"

"I do not expect you to understand the intricacies of business – or the realities of plantation life. I have already told you that I follow my father's commitment to fair treatment of the slaves. And without work on the plantations how would they support their families?"

Annoyed by Charles' patronizing tone Lizzie challenged, "Like you I have never visited a plantation, but I have heard many reliable accounts from Uncle James and Zachary Macaulay and …"

"You have already made your opinions clear! It is obvious that your first loyalty remains with your father! You are far more like him than I realized!"

"If only that were true. He is a better man than anyone else I know!"

"That is not surprising. You have lived your whole life under the constraints of his extreme religious views!"

"You do not know him at all! Even now he is full of life. He lives imprisoned in a brace for his back, in constant pain, and yet his spirit is free!"

"What mere mortal could compete with such a heroic saint!"

"And what of your allegiance to your father?" Lizzie challenged. "You claim that he treated his slaves fairly, yet you employ a man like Stuart!"

"Stuart takes orders from Vincent Bartley, who has proven his reliability for many years!"

"Reliability? How do you really know what goes on across the ocean? You have seen how Stuart behaves with that young girl. What makes you think he would treat your slaves any better?"

An involuntary expression of disgust flitted across Charles' face before he replied, "I have written Vincent a firm letter of instruction to accompany Stuart on his upcoming return voyage."

"A letter?" Lizzie shook her head sadly. "Of course. Now your conscience is clear!"

Charles jerked his head back as if he had been slapped, then replied in an icy tone, "It appears that you have made your decision."

Heart pounding, Lizzie stared back at him as tears stung her eyes. The moment had come. The path forked before her, and she had to make her choice. She held the jeweled dagger in her hands. The dagger that would sever her from the fantasy world where conflicting dreams could coexist peacefully together.

Grasping the pendant of the sapphire necklace, she stroked its smooth surface with her finger. Unlike the brooch that she had worn for so many years, when she wore the necklace, she felt beautiful and desirable, and that nothing else mattered. But now she was finally ready to face the truth that it did not belong to her.

As she undid the clasp of the necklace, she was pierced by the pained expression on Charles' face. "Charles, I hope that you understand," she said gently as she handed it to him. "My longing for a life with you has been so intense that I deceived myself – and you. I forgot who I really am. But we both know the truth. What began as an enchanted encounter under the stars would end with us tearing one another apart."

He stared down at the necklace, and when he looked up his expression was guarded. Stiff. Hard to read. She wished there were something that she could say that would allow them to part as friends, but she knew that was unlikely. And she suspected that his pride was bruised by the rejection of what he had offered more than by regret at losing her.

He stood in silence, his muscles rigid, clenching the necklace in his hand. And so, without another word, she turned away from him, walked toward the door, and did not look back.

Chapter 34

Charles knew it was a mistake as soon as he stepped into the carriage, but he did not care. His mind was reeling with a jumble of conflicting emotions. His body so tense and restless that he had to get out of the house.

Visiting Stuart in this state of mind was not a good idea, but Charles needed a distraction from the choking anger coiled in his chest. Anger at Wilberforce and Lizzie's family. Anger at Lizzie for rejecting his offer. For challenging his choices. His priorities. And although he would prefer to deny it, a vague sense of anger toward himself.

Despite his plan for a meeting at his office before Stuart sailed at the end of the week, Charles needed a pretext for his impromptu evening call. And so, he signed the letter to Vincent, sealed it and added it to the package of documents that he had prepared for Stuart to deliver.

Rowdy strains of piano music filtered into the hall from Stuart's flat. When Rebecca opened the door wearing a low-cut silk negligee that clung to every curve of her body, Charles responded with a surge of desire. She looked up at him with a seductive smile, now well versed in the world of men. When Charles caught Stuart's eyes on him, he looked away abruptly, irritated by Stuart's uncanny powers of observation.

"Come in Charles. Make yourself comfortable," Stuart invited pleasantly as he got up from the piano and walked over to a sideboard with a large collection of bottles. "You look like you need a drink. Brandy? Scotch?

Claret?"

"Brandy," Charles replied as he sat in an overstuffed chair near the fireplace. "I hope I did not come at an inconvenient time," he added, glancing at Rebecca. "I had business nearby, so I decided to drop off the documents for Vincent."

Stuart projected the demeanor of a congenial host and appeared to accept the excuse at face value. "How thoughtful of you Charles. I would have been more than happy to come by your office to pick them up, but this does save me time." With a sweeping gesture he added, "As you can imagine I have been very busy preparing for my voyage."

Charles looked around the room, perplexed at the lack of any signs of preparation. There were no crates or boxes. No luggage. Shelves were still full of books and ornaments. A set of fine china was displayed in an oak cabinet.

A familiar voice emerged from behind a closed door. "Rebecca! What is taking you so long? Come back to bed!"

Rebecca, who had disappeared behind some curtains into another room, walked quickly across the room. But before she reached the door, Stuart interrupted. "Gerald, we have a visitor. Come join us!"

"Give me a minute," Gerald replied, his voice muffled and tinged with frustration. When he emerged a few minutes later, still buttoning up his shirt, an unmade bed was visible behind him.

"Charles," he smiled, without a trace of embarrassment. "I did not realize you were coming." And then, with brashness that Charles found deeply offensive he added, "You look like you need Rebecca far more than I do now Charles. I will gladly defer ..."

"That is not why I came!" Charles retorted. "I thought Rebecca was ... with ... Stuart."

"I want to make sure that she has some patrons to look after her when I leave," Stuart smiled benignly, putting his arm around Rebecca's waist. "A few men of quality and breeding who will pay the rent on this apartment and look after her needs ... Otherwise I hate to think where she might end up!"

"There are three of us so far, including Arthur and Cameron, friends of Stuart's who prefer to avoid the unsavoury aspects of the usual sources of male entertainment," Gerald explained. "But you are welcome to join us."

"Does your wife know about your ... activities?" Charles asked, masking his distaste.

"Of course, she does not ask, but I think the arrangement suits her very well. Her life is full, with afternoon teas and entertaining guests and four active children. And she has made it clear that she does not want any more ..."

Charles made no comment, aware that many successful men kept mistresses. And after all, it was none of his business what Gerald did in his private life, as long as he continued to perform well at work.

"Gerald, you are being insensitive," Stuart chided as he replenished Charles' glass. "Miss Wilberforce may not yet be accepting of such an arrangement."

Charles sipped his drink in silence, unsure what to reveal about Lizzie. He did not trust either Stuart or Gerald to keep anything he shared in confidence, but perhaps he could use them to control the narrative. To spread gossip that would be favourable for his reputation – particularly to his colleagues at the West India Association, who were anticipating a different outcome. "I have disappointing news about Miss Wilberforce," he confided. "I have called off the engagement. A question of priorities. Of loyalty ..."

"A difficult decision no doubt Charles," Stuart replied, "but perhaps for the best." As he poured another glass of brandy he added, "The offer still stands. Rebecca could comfort you in ways that would dispel any regrets about Miss Wilberforce."

Charles was feeling the effects of the brandy and when Rebecca came over and began gently massaging the tight muscles in his neck and shoulders, he wanted more than anything to accept Stuart's offer. And why not, he told himself. If there were any time when he needed the kind of comfort that Rebecca could provide, it was today. He closed his eyes and could feel himself falling under her spell - his body aroused, and ready to yield to her charms.

But when he opened his eyes, Stuart was watching him with barely concealed enjoyment. And jolted to reality, Charles shook off the mellow haze of intoxication and stood up unsteadily. "It is getting late Stuart. I did not intend to stay so long."

During the carriage ride home Charles drifted into a melancholy mood, his mind restive with memories of Lizzie. When he had met her at the Twelfth Night gala – dancing with peasants and pelting him with snowballs – he had known that she was not like other women he knew. Her preference for simple pleasures rather than the pretentions of elite society. Her honesty and directness. Her empathy and strong convictions. Her passion ... These were qualities that had attracted him – and that ultimately drove them apart.

When he entered the house, a thought came to him that diverted him from his pensive mood. Taking a lamp from a table in the main hallway he walked quickly up the stairs to the library. As he studied the architect's drawings, he replayed Lizzie's words. She had said the proposed mansion was ostentatious. She had questioned Charles' motives. His father's legacy. His political ambitions.

Pushing aside the designs, Charles walked over to the large window that faced the harbour and gazed out at the ships silhouetted against the horizon. One of them belonged to him and would soon sail for Nevis and other West Indian ports with a cargo of goods for trade. To return several weeks later filled with sugar – the white gold on which his fortune depended.

When he finally went to bed sleep was elusive, until he fell into a restless dream. He was the captain of a ship tossed by giant waves, in the midst of a stormy sea. The howling wind that battered the ship echoed with frightened voices. Voices crying for help. For relief. For justice. But with a powerful grip on the wheel Charles kept the ship on course until the voices faded away.

Chapter 35

Man on the dubious waves of error toss'd, his ship half founder'd and his compass lost, sees as far as human optics may command, a sleeping fog and fancies it dry land.

The stanza from Cowper's poem echoed in Lizzie's mind during the carriage ride home, distracting her from the sadness that threatened to overwhelm her. But with Ann's kind eyes upon her, she held back her tears and focused on the poem. The image of the ship lost at sea with no compass was an apt description of Charles, she thought bitterly. His lofty ambitions. His skewed priorities. His insatiable drive to acquire more wealth.

But as she rehearsed Charles' faults, she had to admit that she had only herself to blame. Charles had never hidden who he was from her. She had been foolish enough, despite her denials, to imagine that she could reform him. And as she had placed her hopes for happiness on an illusory "sleeping fog," she had lost her way.

When they reached home, Lizzie declined her mother's offer to warm up her dinner and locked herself in her room. Grasping the cameo of Charles from her dressing table, she threw herself onto her bed and allowed her tears to fall without restraint. Grieving for her shattered dreams she sobbed convulsively until exhaustion overtook her, and she fell into a fitful sleep.

She awoke feeling disoriented, still clutching the cameo. The room was in darkness, and when she lit a lamp the small clock on her dresser read twenty minutes past two. As her muddled thoughts cleared, she was gripped with a disquieting sense of apprehension. Too anxious to go back to sleep, Lizzie wrapped a shawl around her nightgown and tiptoed down the back stairs, and out into the garden.

The rain had stopped, leaving behind a dense shroud of mist. When she began to walk along the flagstone path Lizzie stepped into a puddle, soaking her slippers and the bottom of her nightgown. Tossing aside her slippers and her shawl, she began to run along the path, purposely splashing in the puddles – finding release in the shock of cold water on her legs.

When she reached the fishpond at the far end of the small garden, she gazed at the flashes of gold in its depths, soothed by the serenity of this alien world. She could feel the cameo still clenched in her hand, and when she opened her fist, her heart constricted at the portrait of Charles that had been painted for her. His deep blue eyes. The highlights of red in his wavy hair. His disarming smile …

As her breath caught in her throat, she knew what she must do. His image brought back too many memories. When she looked at it the sense of loss was more than she could bear. And so, she gripped the cameo and raised her hand over her head, aiming toward the pond.

But with a pang of grief, she realized that she could not do it. She could not release it into the pond. She was not ready to let go. And with an intense sorrow that she had not felt since the death of her sister, Lizzie fell to her knees and wept.

Chapter 36

Why does he keep watchin' me? Tamar wondered. The grey-haired slave had been unloading supplies for Massa Vincent's big party for over an hour, and every time he passed nearby his eyes would dart furtively toward her. Tamar had never seen him before, but Rachel said he was from the Fitzroy plantation not far down the road.

The house slaves had been busy all morning getting everything set up just right so Massa Vincent would be pleased. And Dinah needed lots of extra help in the kitchen because there were so many fancy dishes to prepare. Tamar had never seen so much food in her life. Hams and roast beef and fancy cheese and candies and fruit tarts and custards and cakes. Such a feast it made her head spin.

And the decorations! Ribbons and bows and special flowers that didn't grow in their garden. And wine and brandy and scotch and a clear bubbly drink Rachel said was called champagne. All because Massa Vincent was getting married in a few weeks.

When Rachel had first told her the news, Tamar had felt a flicker of hope that things would change for her. But when she finally got up the nerve to ask Rachel about it, her reply had been blunt. "A wife won't change nothin' for Massa Vincent. 'Cept maybe he come to your hut 'stead of you comin' to him in his room."

When the old man brought another armload of supplies into the kitchen, he looked like he would say something to Tamar. But then, without a word, he turned around and went out the door for another load.

"He look like he want to say somethin' to me. What you think he want?"

Turning to her oldest son, Rachel instructed, "Daniel, go after that old man. Talk to him on his own and ask what he want with Tamar."

When Daniel returned a few minutes later he blurted, "He say he got a message from Joseph. But he gots to give it to you direct."

Tamar's heart pounded as she tried to make sense of this unexpected news. *Joseph? But how? Where?*

She could see Daniel's curious gaze upon her as he waited for her reply. "Tell him to meet me behind the slave privy. White men don't go there. I'll come soon as I can. And Daniel, I need you to keep watch."

The old man was pacing nervously when Tamar arrived. Glancing around to make sure no one was watching, he spoke in a barely audible voice. "Joseph want you to know he's at a plantation not far away. And Massa Fitzroy a good Massa who tell him if he work hard he can earn his freedom. And when he does, he's comin' for you and the boy."

Startled by this news, Tamar could barely take it in. Joseph nearby? With a chance to earn his freedom? He hadn't forgotten her? For a few joyful moments she allowed herself to dream of a hopeful future. Of a time when she and Joseph and Micah would be together again. When they would no longer be slaves ...

But then, her mind was flooded with images. Images that filled her with shame. Images that shattered her foolish daydreams and left them lying in the dust.

"Tell Joseph to forget 'bout me. The Tamar he knew is gone. Ruined. And my Massa's not a good Massa ..."

"But he not 'spectin' that. He said he don't want no other woman."

The words caught in her throat as tears stung her eyes. "Tell him to find another woman. And not to waste his thoughts on me!"

The old man stared at her in confusion, but before he could reply Tamar turned away and escaped back to the kitchen house. When she entered, Rachel's kind eyes radiated concern. "You alright Tamar?"

Tamar's emotions were so raw, so close to the surface that she could only shake her head, not daring to speak them aloud.

Then, with a nod of understanding, Rachel led Tamar to a large pot of cooked potatoes and handed her a masher. And with a sense of relief, Tamar put aside her agitation and focused her frustrated energy on mashing the potatoes into a creamy pulp.

Chapter 37

Highwood Hill – May 1827 - Four weeks later

"If Mother gives me any more mending, I think I shall scream!" Lizzie fumed as she joined her father on a bench in the garden.

Putting down his book he smiled, "She means well."

"Trying to keep me busy," Lizzie nodded.

"We were very worried about you … after …" He looked away awkwardly, his face creased with strain.

It had been a difficult time for all of them. Lizzie's unrelenting headaches. Her melancholy moods. She had been confined to her bed for days at a time, barely able to eat.

"I feel much better now," Lizzie reassured, unconsciously touching the brooch that until recently had been forgotten in the drawer. "Almost back to myself."

"An answer to many prayers," her father replied, tears gleaming in his eyes. He took her hand in his and patted it gently, then asked hesitantly, "Have you thought further about Hannah's suggestion?"

Lizzie smiled at the mention of her godmother, Hannah More. Although she was not married, she kept up a lively correspondence with the young people who were blessed to have her as a mentor and a friend. Her letters were never dry but sparkled with the clever wit and insightful wisdom that had made her a celebrated author.

"She would gladly have me visit. I will never forget the time that Barbara and I spent with her and her sisters, learning about their work among poor children at the Mendip schools. Hannah is such a good storyteller that her lessons kept the children spellbound."

"I always enjoy my visits there as well. I was particularly struck by the impact on illiterate peasants, who read for the first time at the Sunday schools that they started."

"I feel drawn to work among the poor," Lizzie affirmed. "I just do not know yet whether to join Hannah at Mendip, or to become involved closer to home."

"Perhaps it is good to begin slowly with something nearby until you are ... fully ... recovered."

Fully recovered? Lizzie mused. *Will I ever really heal completely?* Her grief was less acute, and thoughts of Charles no longer consumed her. But would the ache of loss ever go away?

Reaching into a pocket, Lizzie took out the cameo of Charles, and gazed at it uncertainly. Then, setting aside her ambivalence, she held it out to her father. "Could you keep this for me?"

"Are you sure?" he probed gently as he took it from her.

"I do not need any reminders."

With an expression of deep concern, her father stood and took her hand in his. When she stood up, he linked his arm through hers and they began to stroll along the path.

"I am sorry for the way things ended ..." he said gently.

Lizzie was briefly silent, then before her thoughts could drift once more to a melancholy place she replied, "And yet ... He introduced me to a part of myself ..."

"Was she what you expected?"

Lizzie stood still and stared at her father, then with a self-conscious smile she admitted, "Demanding ... capricious ... self-absorbed ... enchanting ..."

"I recall a similar encounter ..." her father smiled.

They strolled a few more steps until Lizzie began to laugh. "A naïve child, lost in her dreams ... A vain prima donna, craving the lime-light ..."

Echoing her laughter he asked, "Have you sent her away?"

"No. But she must learn to share the stage ... To let the others play their parts ..."

"An epic journey for all of us!"

"'How easy it is for the proper false in women's waxen hearts to set their forms ...'"

"Not women only."

"No." Lizzie smiled.

Suddenly their conversation was interrupted by a small energetic boy with a noisy dog close at his heels. "Aunt Lizzie, we've come for a visit. And we're going to stay for a whole week!" Waving a fistful of blooms he added, "I picked some flowers from your garden!"

"They are beautiful William," Lizzie smiled, giving him a big hug. Then, with an elfish grin she whispered in his ear, pointing out the wilted flowers in his grandfather's buttonholes. Standing on his tiptoes William was still too small to reach them until the frail old man bent toward him. After removing the faded flowers, William handed them to Lizzie, then proudly replaced them with fresh blooms. When he had finished his task, he beamed up at her with an expression that melted her heart.

The peaceful moment was interrupted by the voice of Mrs. Knowles. "Miss Lizzie, your mother is looking for you."

Lizzie shook her head in resignation. *Not more mending,* she frowned. *Or worse yet, organizing the attic ...*

But then her father came to her aid. "Tell Mrs. Wilberforce that Lizzie and William are helping me with an errand."

Warmed by her father's mischievous smile Lizzie quipped, "Still setting captives free?"

And then, with a final glance at the wilted flowers, Lizzie tossed them aside and allowed herself to be led along the path to freedom by the laughter and high spirits of two of the people she loved most in the world.

Chapter 38

Pinney Plantation, Nevis – June 1827

"What you think Massa Stuart buy me?" Ruthie exclaimed as she skipped excitedly around the kitchen. "He must have lots of presents in those big boxes!"

"Shush Ruthie," Rachel scolded. "You can't 'spect Massa Stuart to bring you a present."

"But Mama, he always bin nice to me. He give me sweets when he visit you. Sometimes even a pretty ribbon …"

"Ruthie not another word about Massa Stuart!" Rachel snapped. "Now off you go and get those strawberries for Dinah."

Ruthie glared at her mother with disgruntled defiance in her honey-brown eyes, then stomped noisily out the door to the garden.

Tamar glanced over at Rachel in concern. Since the unexpected arrival of Massa Stuart that afternoon, a frenzy of activity had gripped the household. Tobias and Isaac had been busy hauling luggage up the stairs and getting it all unpacked, while Rachel and Tamar were helping Dinah and Becky in the kitchen. But Rachel had been unusually quiet. Distracted. Even irritable.

"You alright?" Tamar whispered as they began to dish up the food to serve the evening meal.

Shaking her head Rachel replied, "You got to wait on them for me Tamar. I can't today."

And so, Tamar's first glimpse of Massa Stuart was over a tray of steaming sweet potato soup. Despite his yellow hair and handsome face, there was something about him that made her uncomfortable. When he looked up at her she finally understood Rachel's distress. His eyes, like Ruthie's, were an unusual shade – like the colour of honey.

The expression on his face made her feel sick inside. "Who is this, Vincent? A new acquisition?"

"Yes. And do not get any ideas in your head of winning her in a game of dice! I will not share her. Not yet anyway."

"I have always enjoyed my visits to Esther in the field slave quarters," Massa Stuart replied with an ugly smirk on his face.

"You left her in the family way before your voyage. Her whelp should be born soon."

"Rachel has always been serviceable at such times," Massa Stuart laughed. "And she has not lost her looks."

Tamar returned to the kitchen house, desperate to avoid the degrading conversation. But there were more dishes to serve for the main course, and she caught snatches of their discussion as she went back and forth.

"Did you have a chance to read Charles' letter?"

"Yes. Quite a document."

"So earnest. So naïve," laughed Massa Stuart.

"And are the crates really full of Slave Bibles?"

"Yes, enough for the entire district!"

"The slaves may not be able to read, but I'm sure they will find some use for the paper!"

What they talkin' 'bout? Tamar wondered. *Are they makin' fun of Massa Pinney?* The two men continued to tease and joke, but Tamar could not make any sense of it at all and was relieved to escape back to the kitchen after placing the last dish on the table.

Ruthie had returned and was perched on a stool chatting to Dinah as she put final touches on the strawberry shortcake.

"Daniel's old enough to understand 'bout Massa Stuart," Rachel murmured to Tamar. "And Amos is startin' to ask questions. But Ruthie, she too young … She don't know …"

Tamar nodded in sympathy, linked by a bond that did not need words.

"If Massa Stuart come tonight," Rachel whispered, her face creased with worry, "I got to send the children out …"

"Of course," Tamar responded. "They's welcome to come to me. Just send them whenever you need to."

Micah was already asleep that evening when there was a knock at the door. Daniel and Amos entered quietly and barely said a word. But Ruthie bounced into the room waving the pretty yellow ribbon that Massa Stuart had brought for her. As she prattled happily about how kind he was to her and to her Mama, Tamar listened with a sad smile, hoping that the high-spirited little girl could be sheltered from the truth for as long as possible.

Chapter 39

Pinney Plantation, Nevis – July 1828 – 1 Year Later

Massa Pinney had looked very angry when he called Massa Vincent and Massa Stuart into the office. His voice was loud, and he had talked to them the way the overseer scolded disobedient slaves. And they had obeyed right away, without any backtalk or joking around.

Curious about the meaning of this unusual meeting, Tobias and Isaac hovered in the hallway near the office as much as they dared, and when it was safe, they sneaked out to the kitchen house to report to the women, who were too busy cooking the midday meal to leave.

"They sure talkin' a lot," Tobias reported. "Hard to hear everthin' they sayin' though."

"Massa Pinney say he not happy with the way they's spendin' money," Isaac continued. "He say the numbers don't add up right."

"And he say they not good massas," Tobias added. "They not behavin' the way they should."

"What Massa Vincent and Massa Stuart sayin'?" Tamar asked. "Are they givin' a lot of 'scuses?"

"When they start talkin' Massa Pinney just tell 'em to shut up and listen!"

Tamar was amazed that anyone could tell those two men to shut up and get away with it. But Massa Pinney was their Massa, and they were supposed to obey him.

When Massa Pinney had arrived a couple of weeks before, the house slaves had not known what to expect from him. He had never been there before, and only Isaac was old enough to remember what his father had been like. Massa Vincent and Massa Stuart had been real nice – smiling a lot and telling him plenty of lies about how good they were to the slaves. And they had left Rachel and Esther and Tamar alone. But when Massa Pinney was not around, they made jokes about him, and said he had come to visit because of a woman who told him she didn't want to marry him - that he wanted to get away from all the gossip.

Massa Vincent's new wife had put on her prettiest dress and invited her fancy friends over for a party for Massa Pinney. And then he got invited back to parties and picnics and dances that kept him too busy to pay much attention to what was happening on the plantation.

But a couple of days ago Massa Fitzroy came for a visit. And he and Massa Pinney had a long talk in the office with the door closed. After he left, Massa Pinney shut himself in the office with a pile of papers and ledgers, and had Rachel bring him his meals on trays.

Ruthie's cheerful voice interrupted Tamar's reverie as she bounced into the kitchen carrying a 3-month-old infant. "Rose been real good Mizz Tamar. But now she want her Mama."

Tamar looked down at the child's sweet face as she held her to her breast. She could never have imagined that she could feel so much love for a baby conceived in such misery. Rose suckled contentedly, looking up with clear green eyes, her face so like her mother's. Tamar was thankful that there was not a trace of her father visible in this child that so filled her heart.

Tobias rushed back into the kitchen, followed by Isaac. "Massa Pinney yellin' at Massa Vincent and Massa Stuart real loud. I think they gon' come out soon!"

Tamar exchanged glances with Dinah and Rachel and Becky, unsure whether they dared to leave the kitchen to see for themselves what would happen next. Then, setting aside her fears, Tamar handed Rose over to Ruthie, and followed the others the few steps across the yard to the house, where they hid close enough to hear the men when they came out of the office, without being seen.

A few minutes later Tamar heard Massa Pinney fling open the office door, and shout, "You have until tomorrow morning to pack up your things and leave this plantation! And you are not welcome to return to this property ever again!"

"But where will we go? What will we do?" whined Massa Vincent.

"That is your concern not mine. I'm sure you will land on your feet. You will no doubt take advantage of your wife's family and social connections."

But then Massa Stuart started yelling at Massa Pinney. "You're so self-righteous Charles! So smug! Where would you be without your father's riches ...?"

"Be quiet Stuart!" Massa Vincent interrupted. "We still have to live on this island!"

But Massa Stuart wouldn't keep his mouth shut. "Just a weak man who depends on others to get their hands dirty so you can keep yours clean! Not man enough to satisfy the Abolitionist's daughter!"

"Get out of my sight! Now!" Massa Pinney shouted.

With her heart thumping into her throat, Tamar peered around the corner, just in time to see Massa Vincent and Massa Stuart stomp angrily up the stairs to their rooms and bang their doors behind them.

* * *

Tamar did not even try to hide her feelings as she met Massa Vincent's angry glare with a triumphant smile. Massa Pinney had allowed all the house slaves to line up on the front verandah to watch the departure of the disgraced men, and it was a day they would never forget. Tamar did feel pity for Massa Vincent's wife, who appeared dazed at the sudden change of her circumstances and was perhaps becoming aware for the first time of the terrible choice she had made when she married him.

The carriage was barely out of sight down the lane when Tobias came to Tamar with a message. "Massa Pinney want to see you in his office right away."

What Massa Pinney want with me? Tamar wondered. *Is he upset 'bout us listenin' in yesterday? Or about Rose? Did Massa Vincent say somethin'?*

When Tamar knocked on the office door Massa Pinney replied, "Come in Tamar and close the door behind you."

As Tamar stood nervously waiting for him to look up from the paper he was reading, anxious thoughts flitted through her mind. *What he want? Is he gon' want me to come to him like Massa Vincent did? Or does he think I'm not doin' a good job? Will he send me back to the fields? Or did Micah do somethin' ...*

"Tamar, I had a long conversation with Mister Fitzroy a few days ago. He has a reputation of being a fair and honest man, and he brought some things to my attention that surprised me."

Massa Fitzroy? What he have to do with me? Tamar wondered, uncomfortable with the Massa's serious eyes upon her.

"He told me about how you came here, to this plantation. That you were separated from your husband."

Tamar stared back at him, tears welling in her eyes. Awkward in his presence, she nodded wordlessly and looked away.

"Mister Fitzroy told me that your husband Joseph has been trying to earn enough to buy freedom for himself, and for you and your son."

"Yes, Massa," Tamar replied, wide-eyed with surprise that he knew of Joseph's plan. "But I send him a message to forget 'bout me ..."

Holding up his hand, Massa Pinney cut short her protests. "Tamar, it would take years for Joseph to earn enough to buy freedom for the three of you. But an injustice has been done that my father would never have allowed. And it is time for me to make it right."

"I don't understand, Massa Pinney. What you sayin'?"

"Mister Fitzroy has agreed to sell Joseph to me, so that he can work here on this plantation. So that your family can be together again."

Tamar was completely overwhelmed and could not speak at all. The feelings that whirled through her mind battled with one another, leaving her in a state of utter confusion. Joy and hope. Shame and fear of rejection. And for a moment she forgot where she was.

"Tamar, I know this is a lot to take in. Joseph will arrive tomorrow morning and you may take the day off to spend with him."

Tamar's emotions were in such turmoil that she did not even remember walking back to her hut. Her mind was flooded with memories of Joseph. Micah would be so excited, and she could barely wait until the next day to see him again. But in the back of her mind lurked a niggling fear. What would Joseph do when he saw Rose? And so, she grabbed hold of the hope that had begun to grow inside of her, and stuffed it back down where it belonged.

* * *

"I can see the wagon Mama!" Micah shouted, spinning with excitement. "Papa's here!" Without waiting for her reply the small boy began to run down the lane calling "Papa! Papa!"

Tamar's heart swelled when Joseph jumped down from the wagon, picked Micah up and swung him around in his strong arms. When he put him down, Micah chattered happily as they walked hand in hand the rest of the way.

Tamar fidgeted nervously as they approached, longing to run into Joseph's arms, but knowing she no longer belonged there. Joseph stopped a few feet away and searched her face. Then with a tender smile he strode forward and grasped her hands.

With her heart pounding in her chest, she pulled away and shook her head. "Joseph things is not like they was. I'm glad you here for Micah. But the Tamar you knew is gone."

"What you sayin' Tamar? I's here now. We can be a family again."

Aware that Micah was listening intently to every word, Tamar turned to him and instructed, "Micah, go to the kitchen house and fetch those cinnamon buns that Aunt Dinah makin'. Somethin' special for Papa."

Micah smiled up at his parents, then ran as fast as his short legs could take him to complete his important assignment.

Tamar was conscious of the weight of Rose, sleeping in a sling on her back. Untying the sling, she pulled the infant into her arms, her eyes fixed on Joseph's face. "She mine Joseph. Her name is Rose."

As he stared at the child with a startled expression, Rachel's stomach fluttered, her anxiety worsened by his silence. "Massa Vincent … he a bad Massa … He did things to me … You need to find a new woman …"

Joseph's face tightened in anger and Tamar pulled back, afraid of his response. "When you was taken, I knew why he wanted you," he replied bitterly. "And I'd lie awake at night imaginin' what he doin' to you – and what I'd do to him if I was free."

"He did worse than you could imagine," Tamar replied, her voice barely audible. "That's why I sent that message to forget 'bout me."

"But I can't ever forget you Tamar …"

"I'm dirty … spoiled …" she interrupted, her face contorted with pain.

"No! Massa Vincent never had your heart. And he gone now."

As his eyes settled on Rose, Joseph reached out his hand and stroked her cheek. "She beautiful Tamar. She look just like you." And then, he took the child in his arms and rocked her gently. "She ain't done nothin' wrong. And neither have you!"

Tears stung Tamar's eyes at his words. "But she another man's child. I can't 'spect you to raise her as your own."

Placing a finger on her lips, he silenced her protests, then put his free arm around her. "Tamar, I bin' waitin' a long time. You and Micah – and Rose – you'se my family."

Micah's eager shouts ended the conversation. "Papa! Mama! Aunt Dinah give us lots and lots of cinnamon buns," he grinned, lugging a basket that was almost too big for him. With a huge smile Joseph handed Rose back to Tamar. Then with one hand he grabbed the basket, while with the other he swung Micah up onto his shoulders. And then, turning to Tamar he held out his hand and urged, "Tamar, let's go home.

* * *

Rachel had taken Micah and Rose to the kitchen house to give Joseph and Tamar some time alone. But when Joseph embraced her, Tamar's body was rigid with shame, her mind assaulted with ugly images. Releasing her gently, he sat on a stool in the corner of the hut and invited her to join him. As she leaned against him, he massaged the tension from her neck and shoulders as he had done so many times before. They sat in peaceful silence for what seemed like a long time. The familiar routine was soothing, the beginning of the healing of her soul that she so desperately needed.

It was a routine that became part of the rhythm of their lives over the following days and weeks. Tamar longed for things to return to the way they had been between them, wondering if the walls she had built to protect her heart would ever come down.

Then, unexpectedly, one evening as Joseph stroked her neck, Tamar's resistance was swept away in a surge of desire. She pulled him down onto the straw mattress, knowing that his nails, unlike Massa Vincent's, were dirty and torn. His hands rough and calloused. And that when he touched her, they would be gentle.

Chapter 40

Camp House, Clifton – Bristol, England – August 3, 1833

"He inspires more love and veneration than ever fell to the lot of any civilised individual throughout the civilized globe ..." Charles frowned as he perused yet another article about the virtue and heroic career of the man who for so long had been a threat to the prosperity of Bristol, and to his own fortune. The timing of Wilberforce's death three days after the passage on July 26 of the Bill for Abolition of Slavery In The British Colonies had, of course, magnified the sense of drama. And in an unusual display of solidarity, over a hundred influential figures, including both Whig and Tory MPs, and the Lord Chancellor, had written to request that Wilberforce be buried in Westminster Abbey after the funeral, which was to take place that afternoon.

As he continued to read, Charles was piqued by Wilberforce's response to news of the passage of the Abolition Bill. "Thank God that I should have lived to witness the day in which England is willing to give 20 millions sterling for the abolition of slavery."

Setting the newspaper onto an ornate wrought iron table, Charles poured another cup of Earl Grey tea from the teapot and added three cubes of sugar. *Our opponents may have won the vote,* he smiled, *but thanks to the work of the West India Association, slave owners will be well compensated financially, and will benefit from their freed slaves working at minimal cost as apprentices for four more years!*

His wife Frances was standing in front of the gazebo in the middle of the garden, giving instructions to the gardener about how to decorate it for a party that she was planning for her friends. She had adapted well to her role as mistress of the beautiful Clifton house, which had been completed two years earlier, in time for their wedding. She had excellent taste, reflected in the understated elegance with which she was decorating their home, as well as in her fashionable, and very expensive, wardrobe. Her social circle was wide and influential; she was a definite asset to his career.

The first year of their marriage had been tumultuous since his brief tenure as Mayor of Bristol was disrupted by the Bristol riots and charges of neglect of duty. Although his name had been cleared, he was much more realistic about the perils of political involvement, and how quickly the tide of public opinion could shift. Even though prevailing sentiment was now in favour of the abolitionists, it could be fickle. Only time would tell whether this new-found zeal for reform would last.

As Charles sipped his tea, his thoughts turned to Lizzie. *I wonder if she regretted her choice,* he mused. So much time spent doing philanthropic work in the hovels of peasants. Marriage to a poor curate of a small village church, followed by the birth of a daughter and then … Death at the age of 31, just over a year before her father's death. From the same consumption that had cut short her sister's life. *Was it worth it Lizzie?* he frowned. *You threw away all this – and for what?*

Gulping down the last of his tea, he crossed the flagstone terrace and entered the French doors that led up a flight of stairs to his second-floor office. Unlocking the centre drawer of his desk he pulled out a slim volume, which was hidden beneath a ledger, and flipped it open to the dedication inside the front cover. "To Charles – a reminder of that magical Twelfth Night under the stars. Yours, Lizzie."

Shakespeare's Twelfth Night. When Lizzie had given the book to him, just prior to her time away at Rothley, the pages had been smooth and unstained. But now they were worn and creased, the small book a frequent companion whenever she filled his thoughts.

What would she think of Frances? he wondered. *Of this house? Of the Abolition Bill?* He had no doubt about the grief that she would have experienced if her father had died before her.

Closing his eyes, the image returned. Lizzie staring up at him, her face flushed and eyes bright as they danced under the stars. So different from anyone he had ever met. Twelfth Night. A night of celebration, of mystery – and of promise …

"Elizabeth Wilberforce," she had whispered at their next encounter when she *had finally revealed her identity. "It is a name that is too big for me."* And now, her father, who had often been lampooned in cartoons, and reviled by the pro-slavery lobby, would be memorialized in a national shrine.

In the end, as she had warned, their differences were too great. Each tied to a family legacy that pulled them in opposing directions. In the current political climate Charles wondered how the heritage that he had received from his father would impact his family now, and in the future.

As Charles turned the pages of the book, Lizzie's voice echoed through his thoughts. *Do you regret your choices, Charles? Is all your wealth worth it? You threw away the chance to build a different legacy. And for what?* His chest constricted as a jumble of conflicting images and emotions flashed through his mind, revealing the restless discontent that was usually kept at bay by the demands and pleasures of his everyday life.

Closing the book, he put it back in the drawer beneath the ledger. Safely out of sight but never far away. Like his own regrets and longings about what might have been.

Loose The Chains Of Injustice

Is not this the kind of fasting I have chosen:

To loose the chains of injustice and untie the cords of the yoke,

To set the oppressed free and break every yoke?

Is it not to share your food with the hungry and to provide the poor wanderer with shelter –

When you see the naked to clothe them, and not to turn away from your own flesh and blood?

Then your light will break forth like the dawn, and your healing will quickly appear;

Then your righteousness will go before you, and the glory of the Lord will be your rear guard.

Then you will call, and the Lord will answer; you will cry for help and he will say: Here I am.

If you do away with the yoke of oppression, with the pointing finger and malicious talk,

and if you spend yourselves in behalf of the hungry and satisfy the needs of the oppressed,

Then your light will rise in the darkness, and your night will become like the noonday.

The Lord will guide you always; he will satisfy your needs in a sun-scorched land and will strengthen your frame.

You will be like a well-watered garden, like springs whose waters never fail.

Your people will rebuild the ancient ruins and will raise up the age-old foundations;

You will be called Repairer of Broken Walls,

Restorer of Streets with Dwellings.

Isaiah 58: 6 to 12

Epilogue

Bristol, England, June 7, 2020

"Pull it down! Pull it down! Pull it down!" The excited chanting of antiracism protesters continued to grow louder as the hated figure was splashed with red paint and blindfolded. Ropes were then tied around its neck and ankles, and the statue of Edward Colston was pulled from the pedestal where it had stood in a place of honour for well over a century. Homage to a prominent merchant, leader, and philanthropist. A monument to a slave-owner whose fortune was made on sugar plantations in the West Indies.

When it fell into the square with a loud crash, a few bold protesters kneeled on the neck of the lifeless figure – a tribute to George Floyd, whose death 13 days previously had ignited a global movement. There was a carnival atmosphere as the statue was dragged along the road to the wharf. When the bronze figure was dumped into the harbour where his slave ships had docked two centuries earlier, the cheering of the crowd reverberated out to sea – and around the world.

THE END

Dedicated to people from every generation who seek justice and defend the oppressed in big and small ways

Discussion Questions

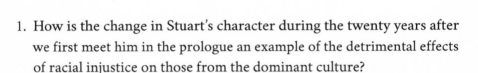

1. How is the change in Stuart's character during the twenty years after we first meet him in the prologue an example of the detrimental effects of racial injustice on those from the dominant culture?

2. In chapter 6 Charles reads an excerpt from his father's journal: "Surely God ordained them (slaves) for the use and benefit of us: otherwise his Divine Will would surely have been made manifest by some particular Sign or Token." What were the underlying motives for this rationalization?

3. Apply Wilberforce's question "Would distance diminish your complicity?" (chapter 8) to a current social issue.

4. In chapter 10 Lizzie says to her father, "Like Viola in Twelfth Night, disguising herself as a man … I dressed in borrowed garments … I was the Liberator's daughter. Clothed in your reputation, I never doubted my zeal." Discuss the conflicting roles that Lizzie experiences.

5. Respond to Stuart's assertion in chapter 11 that "… the true religion in this country is business and trade. Profit and greed its primary virtues! Poverty and privation its only sins."

6. How do you view James Stephen's challenge to Lizzie in chapter 19: "I've met many stunted souls who make truth and goodness look dull because their motive is duty, not love. They're cloaked in self-righteousness, but it scarcely hides their bitterness! I'd hate to see you join their ranks."

7. In chapter 28 Tamar notices Styles, one of Vincent's guests, who seems uncomfortable, perhaps even ashamed, with the crude way the other men are treating her, and yet remains passive. Discuss how this passivity in the face of injustice might apply to contemporary situations.

8. In chapter 30 Stuart baits Charles by drawing attention to the "Slave Bible." How do you respond to the way Christian faith was sometimes distorted so that it would serve the agenda of the rich and powerful?

9. Although Joseph is a strong and capable man, he is powerless to protect his wife and child when his family is torn apart. What are more recent effects of racial injustice on families?

10. In chapter 40, we see how differently Lizzie's and Charles' lives turn out. "Lizzie's voice echoed through his thoughts. Do you regret your choices, Charles? Is all your wealth worth it? You threw away the chance to build a different legacy. And for what?" Who do you think made the better life choice? Why?

11. Charles and other successful merchant slaveowners funded their philanthropy with money earned from the unpaid work of slaves. Why do you think they did this?

12. Discuss how the toppling of the statue of Edward Colston is an example of the importance of understanding the historical roots of current injustices.

13. William Wilberforce and his Abolitionist colleagues worked for over 20 years before the bill that ended the British Slave Trade was passed in 1807. It then took another 26 years before the Emancipation bill that freed existing slaves in the West Indies was passed in 1833. How do you respond to this remarkable example of persistence in fighting injustice?

Afterword

Hearts Of Wax is inspired by the true story of the family crisis that resulted in 1827 when Lizzie Wilberforce became engaged to Charles Pinney, a merchant from Bristol who had inherited several plantations on Nevis, in the West Indies, from his father, John Pretor Pinney. Although I have tried to be as faithful as possible to the historical characters and events, many scenes use creative imagination and dramatic license to convey the story. All dialogue has been created, except for an excerpt from the journal of Charles' father in Chapter 6, William Cowper's poem, the content of the letter from John Wesley to Wilberforce in Chapter 15, and the words of William Cobbett in chapter 32, which are all widely available in books and online articles. A letter from Barbara Wilberforce to one of Charles Pinney's sisters, in Chapter 27, is paraphrased from Anne Stott's book (see below.) The quotation concerning Wilberforce in Chapter 40 is from MyLearning.org. A stanza from Shakespeare's *Twelfth Night* is also quoted in several places. The passages from Isaiah 58 and Isaiah 1: 17 are from the New International Version of the Bible.

Historical characters include William and Elizabeth Wilberforce, and other members of the Wilberforce family, Charles Pinney and his sisters, as well as James Stephen, Tom Macaulay and Thomas and Jean Babington. All other characters, including Stuart Knight, Vincent Bartley, Malcolm and Lydia Bartley, Tamar, Joseph, Rachel, and the other slaves are fictional. **Although in the current social climate there is some risk involved when a white author attempts to write from the perspective of black characters,**

152

particularly slaves from another era who suffered horrific abuse, I felt that it would be a further act of injustice not to give them a voice.

Historical Background

Hearts Of Wax takes place in 1827, two years after the retirement of William Wilberforce from a long career as a British Member of Parliament. He was already an MP when he converted to Christianity in his late twenties, after a trip to Europe with Isaac Milner. His conversion led to a significant struggle about whether he should remain in politics. One of the men who helped him to see his role of MP as an opportunity to serve God was former slave ship captain turned Abolitionist preacher John Newton, author of the hymn Amazing Grace. Wilberforce was later recruited to the cause of Abolition by Lady Middleton, and joined with other colleagues including Thomas Clarkson, James Ramsay, Zachary Macaulay, Henry Thornton, and James Stephen in the town of Clapham to form an anti-slavery society later known as the Clapham Sect. Together they worked for twenty years, despite significant opposition, until the Abolition of the Slave Trade Act was passed in England on February 23, 1807. Ironically, slavery had been illegal in England itself for many years before that. Wilberforce and his colleagues then worked for Emancipation, to set free existing slaves in British colonies, which did not come into effect until 1833. Wilberforce died three days later, on July 29, 1833, finally able to depart in peace, and was buried in Westminster Abbey.

Wilberforce had been a mediocre student at university, apart from a love of the Greek classics, wasting much of his time at social events and playing cards. After his conversion he remained very sociable, with well-known wit and humour. He tended to be disorganized and to procrastinate, yet during his life accomplished an amazing amount. He supported many different causes, including prison reform, abolition of child labour, and prevention of cruelty to animals. Weak eyesight was a problem all his life, becoming worse with age. Although this affected his work, he managed to write thousands of letters by hand to friends and constituents. He spent a great amount of time encouraging his friends in this way. He was very sensitive in character and suffered physically with a chronic bowel condition when faced with difficult decisions and political stresses. His kindness to his opponents and ability to see both sides of an issue sometimes made him appear indecisive. In later life Wilberforce developed a curvature of the spine and lived in a steel girdle cased in leather with an additional part to support the arms for the last 15 or 18 years of his life but did not complain. He was only thankful for having a device that was so helpful to him. Dorothy Wordsworth, wife of poet William Wordsworth, was a friend of the Wilberforce family. In the summer of 1818, the Wilberforce family visited the Wordsworths and "after being a close neighbour for six weeks, (Mrs. Wordsworth) decided, 'There never lived on earth, I am sure, a man of sweeter temper than Mr. Wilberforce. He is made up of benevolence and loving-kindness, and though shattered in constitution and feeble in body, he is as lively and animated as in the days of his youth.'" (*Wilberforce Family And Friends* by Anne Stott, 2012.)

Although Wilberforce was the leader of the abolitionists of the Clapham Sect, using his quick wit and eloquence to present the anti-slavery cause year after year in parliament, he could never have succeeded alone. Thomas Clarkson traveled around 35,000 miles by horseback collecting evidence concerning the Slave Trade to share with his abolitionist colleagues, speaking at anti-slavery meetings and distributing essays. He interviewed 20,000 sailors and several ship surgeons about their experiences on slave ships, and collected implements such as thumbscrews, shackles, and branding irons for display at antislavery meetings. As he began to have more influence, a group of sailors who had been paid to assassinate him nearly killed him, but he continued despite the dangers. James Stephens' direct experience of slavery during the 11 years that he worked in the West Indies as a lawyer fueled his passion to end the Slave Trade and contributed to the evidence that the abolitionists were carefully collecting. His legal expertise was essential in helping to draft the bill for Abolition that was finally successful in 1807. Wilberforce's cousin Henry Thornton, who was also a Member of Parliament, used his wealth to promote Abolition. Battersea rise, his family home, became the focal point that drew several of the others to move to Clapham to facilitate working together. There were many others who made significant contributions, including Zachary Macaulay, Granville Sharp, Lady Middleton and Hannah More, as well as James Ramsay and Olaudah Equiano, a former slave. Josiah Wedgwood used his successful pottery business to create the "Wedgwood Slave Medallion," an image of a kneeling slave in chains embossed with the saying, "Am I not a man and a brother?" The medallions were worn on necklaces, brooches, and hatpins, as well as on items such as snuff boxes, and became a powerful symbol of the antislavery movement.

According to an August 2021 New Yorker article called Home Truth by Sam Knight, Britain's entire economy, particularly in port cities like Bristol, had been heavily dependent on slavery for over two centuries. The Legacy Of British Slavery database that went online in 2013 documents that at the time of Emancipation in 1833 the British government agreed to pay 20 million pounds to compensate slave owners and investors for the "loss of human property," and finally finished paying off the debt in 2015. One in eight Members of Parliament at that time, and a quarter of the directors of the Bank of England, were either directly, or as relatives, recipients of the compensation.

Just as disturbing were the distortions in theology that allowed respectable people who considered themselves Christians to rationalize owning and mistreating other humans who, like them, were made in the image of God. Even the Archbishop of Canterbury received 9000 pounds for the loss of 411 slaves.

The book *Wilberforce Family And Friends* by Anne Stott is an excellent resource which gives detailed background about William Wilberforce and his family, as well as concerning several of his abolitionist colleagues. Although several other books about William Wilberforce and other abolitionists provided helpful information, Stott's book was the major source for *Hearts*

Of Wax concerning the relationship between Lizzie Wilberforce and Charles Pinney.

The following excellent articles give concise background on the British Slave Trade, and on the gruelling life of slaves who worked on sugar cane plantations in the West Indies:

The History Of British Slave Ownership Has Been Buried: Now Its Scale Can Be Revealed – by David Olusogu, theguardian.com, July 12, 2015

A Speech That Made Abolition History by Bill Coles – Wall Street Journal (WSJ.com) May 12, 2007

History Keeps Account

Although _Hearts Of Wax_ is primarily a historical novella, the account of the toppling of Edward Colston's statue, which is described in the epilogue, illustrates how relevant the history of slavery remains for western societies today.

In the book _Be The Bridge_, by Latasha Morrison, which advocates building bridges of racial reconciliation through small groups, the second chapter is called History Keeps Account.

"Historical truths play an important role in our understanding of how we arrived in our current racial tension. Without looking back, without understanding the truth of our history, it's difficult to move forward in healthy ways. And even though it might be painful to recount our history as a country, denying it leads nowhere. Truth is the foundation of awareness, and awareness is the first step in the process of reconciliation. Jesus said as much: 'You shall know the truth, and the truth will make you free.' Truth frees us to grow. Frees us to see. Frees us to be aware. Frees us from the bondage of racial sin. Frees us to have courage for difficult conversations."

Another excellent resource that discusses the importance of facing up to the historical injustices of the past in order to work toward true reconciliation is _Roadmap To Reconciliation 2.0_ by Dr. Brenda Salter McNeil, a black professor of reconciliation studies with over thirty years of experience in racial, ethnic and gender reconciliation.

Seek Justice, Defend the Oppressed

Two centuries after Abolition of the British Slave Trade and Emancipation of existing slaves there are more than 40 million people in slavery today – more than ever before in human history. Modern day slavery includes sex trafficking and cybersex trafficking, forced labour slavery, citizenship rights abuse, police abuse of power and land theft. ***There are still dragons to slay***

Combating slavery requires a variety of approaches, including rescuing victims, bringing criminals to justice, reforming justice systems, and aftercare of survivors. There are several organizations that focus on different aspects of this work, including A21 Campaign, Ally Global, Dressember and International Justice Mission, among others.

Sometimes justice systems themselves need to be reformed, even in North America. *Just Mercy: A Story Of Justice And Redemption* by lawyer Bryan Stevenson powerfully traces the development of the Equal Justice Initiative (eji.org) in the United States which seeks to challenge the bias in the prison system against the poor and people of colour. ***There are still dragons to slay.***

"Learn to do right. Seek justice. Defend the oppressed."
  (Isaiah 1: 17)

Acknowledgements

Although I began to write this novella in September 2020, it is the culmination of a twenty-year journey that included writing a stage play (2003) and a screenplay (2010.) For several years they gathered dust until I decided to rewrite them in a more accessible format. The creative process is a long story that has involved a steep learning curve, with paid and unpaid critiques several years ago by theatre professionals (for which I am grateful to Simon Johnston, Elizabeth Beachy, Dr. Gillette Elvgren, Tonya Diston, Jeremy Tow, Reed Needles, Dennis Hassell, Ron Reed, Ian Farthing and Bryan Coley) as well as many friends and relatives too numerous to name here.

For this novella, I appreciate the input of Kim Cechetto, Elaine Thurgood and Patricia Morley-Forster, who are part of an amateur creative writing group that I attend, as well as feedback from Sue Mitchell, Fran Robinson, Betty-Ann Wilson, Rita Mendis-Mogenson, Shanthal Perera, Sunali Perera, Ron Corcoran, Cynthia Mesikano Kabutha, Bob Kline, Linda Kline, Dennis Funk and Ruth Funk. Wendy M. Wilson has been very helpful in guiding me through the process of self-publishing.

Words seem inadequate to express the many lessons that I have learned from the challenges of writing Hearts Of Wax, and the ways in which it has become interwoven with my own spiritual journey. During difficult seasons in life, when so many things seem out of my control, it is therapeutic to have some control (albeit flawed) over the words on the page! And it is a blessing finally to be able to share this story, which has been on my heart for so many years, in the hope that it will be an encouragement, and that it will, in some

160

small way, bring glory to God.

About The Author

Leslie Ruth (Mogenson) Damude lives in London, Ontario, Canada with her husband, and is blessed to have two adult children and six granddaughters who live nearby. An interest in creative writing, social justice, and community development was stimulated by three years (1985 to 1988) spent in the Democratic Republic Of Congo (then Zaire) as well as experiences during her part-time work as a Family Physician. Retirement in the spring of 2019 has rekindled an interest in creative writing when family responsibilities permit.

In addition to writing Hearts Of Wax, Leslie helped her mother, Ruth Wensley Mogenson, write and self-publish a memoir called *Take My Hands*, which is available on Amazon.

CPSIA information can be obtained
at www.ICGtesting.com
Printed in the USA
LVHW041317140523
746937LV00002B/340